THE MOTHS OF ELENGEN

Eric Franco

Paperback: ISBN: 979-8-9905172-0-2
Edited by: Eric Franco
Cover design by: Eric Franco
Layout by: Eric Franco
Contact Publisher at: contact@akamoth.com
Author Website: akamoth.com

This book is for everyone who keeps the wheels of life turning because without the mundane there would be no Beauty.

My official website is https://www.akamoth.com

"I must create a system or be enslaved by another man's; I will not reason and compare: my business is to create."

—William Blake, Jerusalem: The Emanation of the Giant Albion

THE MOTHS OF ELENGEN

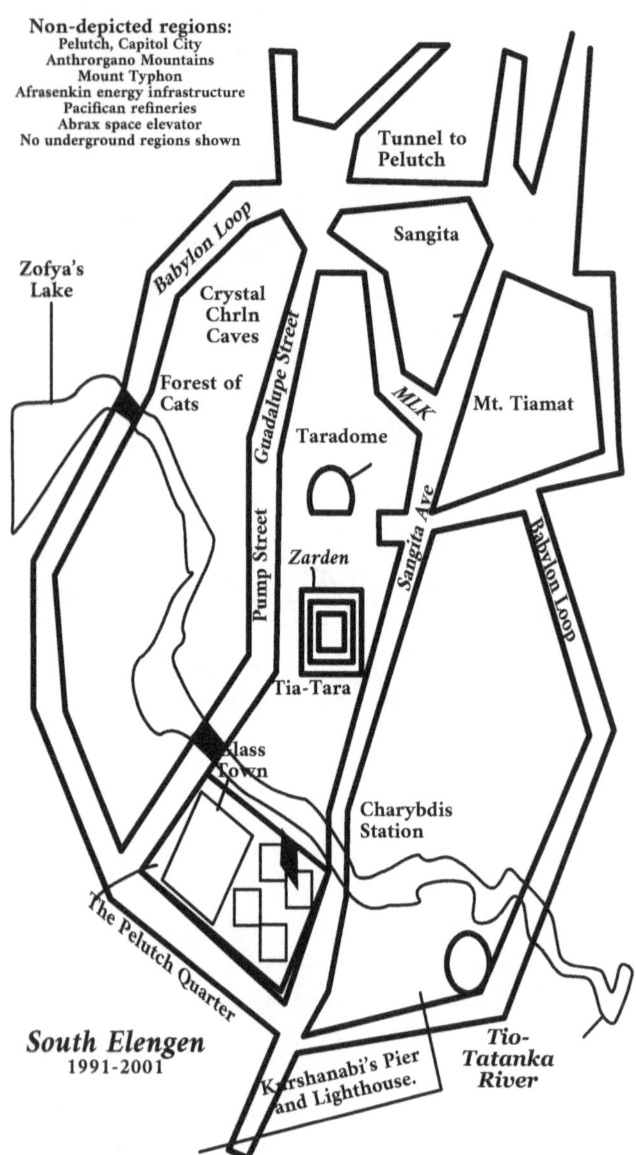

Non-depicted regions:
Pelutch, Capitol City
Anthrorgano Mountains
Mount Typhon
Afrasenkin energy infrastructure
Pacifican refineries
Abrax space elevator
No underground regions shown
Tunnel to Pelutch
Sangita
Zofya's Lake
Babylon Loop
Crystal Chrln Caves
Guadalupe Street
MLK
Mt. Tiamat
Forest of Cats
Taradome
Pump Street
Sangita Ave
Babylon Loop
Zarden
Tia-Tara
Glass Town
Charybdis Station
The Pelutch Quarter
South Elengen
1991-2001
Kurshanabi's Pier and Lighthouse.
Tio-Tatanka River

Elengen was designed and constructed as permaculture minded noosphere for a Post-Human ecosystem which could survive through any environmental hazard or collapse.

This design proposed constructing an artificial island through directed bio-mineralization of coral reefs. This began by seeding a remote area of open ocean covering approximately 150 square kilometers with genetically modified coral organisms that have been selectively engineered and bred to exhibit significantly accelerated growth rates, averaging an increase in size of 20 centimeters in just one year.

This modified coral stock would then be cultivated to rapidly develop an expanding reef structure through focused deposition of calcium carbonate skeletal material as the individual coral polyps flourished and the aggregate reef rose closer to the surface of the waters over decades.

Once the coral reef foundation forms, volcanic vents were triggered within the island to sculpt its shape. The resulting eruptions uplifted rare earth mineral deposits, including an estimated 51 trillion kilograms of neodymium from the impact site of a Saturnian meteorite. Erupting lava flows shaped a central peak, then collapsed to form a caldera in a geothermal hotspot.

Reinforced bio-composite materials introduced into the initial design stages provided stabilized foundations and shoreline protections. Coastal ecosystems gradually became established upon the accumulating coral framework which would ultimately fill in to create dry land through carefully managed biological and mineral processes.

That was how Pelutch in North Elengen came to be. Divided by the Anthrorgano Mountains, South Elengen was a place where the stars could still be seen at night.

—pg. 1.14:16 The People of Pelutch by Hed Remar

Dramatis Personae

Yuza Moth: 29
Zoe Moth: 26
Bastet Moth: 28
Makeda Nysos-Moth: 21
Felicia Rodriguez-Moth (Adopted): 17
Yal Moth (Son of Akachi and Yuza): 15
Spryaig (Son of Akachi and Bastet): 13
Dio Nysos (Son of Akachi and Makeda): 2
Zani Nysos (Daughter of Akachi and Makeda): 1
Gráinne Moth: 50
Akachi: ?

THE MOTHS OF ELENGEN

03/24/1991

My sister Zoe Moth distributed notebooks to everyone in South Elengen awhile back, and I've finally gotten around to writing in my own. She told everyone to choose an imaginary person who you can always write to, someone static, timeless, so I chose to imagine a daughter named Aktaly.

Yalson, my first and only boy is already beyond me, training with obsession to become Manticore, but he ignores Felicia, the youngest Moth who loves him. He has already forgot that fighting for love is what keeps his heart pumping, not fighting fear. Anyway, let's see how this kind of writing works, Aktaly, daughter of my future memory. I'm not going to overthink the format. Goddess knows the Amraken schools would have us think formal speech is the only way to write an international language.

A buzzing mist of damselflies and gnats followed me as I made my way to the compost bio-reactor midway down my local stretch of the Tia-Tara hillock. The net draped from my bun around my body kept our little decomposing helpers from their supper of tamale husks, coffee grounds, plantain peels and olive pits.

The wooden fence posts along the mud and stone staircase slumped in the melting mud; same as all summer, when no critters, only people were mucking about in the musty dreck too thick for boots or fur. We Moths built the hillock ten years back by burying sand packed barrels. The muddy dredges were unfortunately our only means of getting' up and down the hill short of climbing over our neighbor's fences. I'se always a few inches taller from the packed mud under my feet after each trip up and down the hillock.

Iron gates bar the paths to our neighbors on either side of the path. They have personal cisterns and mulching machines in their leveled yards. Their compost gurgled through pipes that ran along the same, melting stone staircase I trudged down. My dainty brown bucket held enough kitchen waste for two trips each afternoon before dark. The light weight helped when I had to step over the rust eaten remains of the trolley track. Decomposing right where it broke down three summers ago.

The bio-reactor deposit box, crafted from an old mailbox was adjacent to several bamboo shacks. The reactor itself was buried underground. Felicia worked the station ahead of me.

"How goes?" I ask while she unwraps the ropes tied along her ruddy myco-fiber backpack.

"Huh? Oh, Yuza, look at this, I couldn't believe it," she pulled out a double plastic wrapped mushroom block riddled with two...three...twelve different colors? *In one block?*

"Never, it makes no sense," I said. "Burn it!"

"This the third time. And its not just us."

"Because you didn't burn it the first two times. Goodness Felicia, Gráinne taught us better."

"She taught *you*," Felicia dropped the mushroom block between us and plodded off, leaving clumps of mud behind her as she began her own trek back up the melting hillside.

"*Bye*."

I set down my bucket, removed my gloves to put on my respirator on then replaced the gloves to pick up the mushroom block. There had to be at least twelve colors: purple, red, indigo, bronze, gold, green, silver, orange, pink, teal, brown, and the rest was gray. I'd seen mutations in the 1970s before, back on the Amraken mainland, and a few times out here, but never something so stable. Usually different bacteria battle each other for territory and overwhelm each other...but here, held in my hands were at the very least twelve different infections...co-existing. And, if Felicia was right, it'd already spread, through the wind most likely, wacky as it'd been with all the Amraken wind turbines along the eastern coast. I decided to ask Gráinne. First though I placed the block inside the drop box. Burning it would make no difference at the rate it had likely already spread.

From midway down the hill, I had a clear view of the tempered pink clouds who were flecked with reddish encroaching storms. Sabaoth, holy sun, try not to scorch us all why don't you? No matter, orange as ever. I think the mist at night is all that keeps our home from igniting. Despite the heat, there have been no fires all year. *Yet anyway.*

I picked up a mud caked garden trowel to scrape some of the mud from my feet and in between my toes. I looked around the shed for a water bucket, but, guess what? Felicia had left it open and that buzzing posse of flies that'd been following me had moved on to a new war for the water.

I spat into the water. The armies of buzzing bugs fluttered for a second before diving back into the fray. I pulled up some grass from around the shed, then sat down on a wooden chair to scrap my the rest of the mud off my feet. If only I had wings none of this would have to be. I could swoon down the hill, drop my load in the bin and soar to some sweeter place, all without touching the mud.

The path to Gráinne's was actually paved. There was a Hispanic man with peppered high and tight hair wearing brown coveralls sweeping the blue and pink brick path clear up ahead. "Hal" he said to me with a wave of his stout, leathery hands.

"Hal, how goes?"

"Beunda."

"Silo."

"Shamai."

"Shamai, shamai," I continued past him.

I stopped at one bend in the path which wrapped around a hillock with Charybdis, the hydro-electric pressure gate carved from the rock into a smooth ravine of white water and smooth boulders which petered out to the beach. Without glasses or binoculars, I could still make out my Yalson among the other boys playing ball near Kurshanabi's lighthouse. He walked with his hips out in front like he's always leaning backward.

Bees flitted from sweet purple hyacinths which grew from the cracks in the white stones of the guard rail. One landed on the back of my gloved hands. I winced and knocked the bee away. I'd touched the infected mushroom block, but left my gloves on. That bee might have just coated themselves with infected spores.

I whispered aloud to *Mother Matter*, "Tia-Sophia, have mercy. Do not blight us yet."

A swoosh of wind rustled some tall, heavy branches of a sycamore which towered above the bend in the paved path. Its roots were the path's foundation after all. No more omens moored over me as I walked the rest of the way to *Taradome*. A few fluttering orange moths followed: *Ruak*.

The stairwell up to the dome was made of full logs, without a single one slumping from the place they were reset ten years ago when our inclined pulley-trolley system still worked.

At the top of the stairs, the leather front door flap was pinned open and a rancor of voices, musical, yet disharmonious leaked out of the entrance to *Taradome*—Tia-Tara Hillock's Geodesic Dome. This was the first structure of our little commune when us Moths migrated here from Amraken in '76. Without any men we managed to assemble the bamboo frame, and grow oyster mushroom blocks and mats to fill all the triangles panels with; we'd tried sedum and peat at first, but that would grow too much so we stuck with hempcrete. What we didn't know at the time was that Amraken smart dust had been mixed into the hempcrete we'd brought with us. What started as clay and wood, glass bottles, tires, solar panels and green hydroponic living walls. Overtime, the dome *grew* ducts, wires, and beeping sensors from the its left side near the Amraken brutish block of a radio transmitter station next to it. Crisp wafts of cedar danced in a black smoky spindle out the chimney of the Taradome. I dropped my dirty gloves into a bin and hoped I wasn't carrying any more spores.

Right before I entered I saw some small toes peeping out from behind the door flap. I peaked around to see Bastet's Son, Spryaig, coiling stripped copper wires around a long steel bolt. His green and yellow clothes looked like they'd been iron pressed and starched before they turned into sweaty rags clinging like moss to his picaresque form.

"Does your Mother know?"

"She's not the boss of me!"

"*Baizan!* Geeze" I said before shaking my head and entering the dome. That boy had been tousled by my Yalson and others too for all their years now. He always had some metal in his hands. But no man would train him how to use weapons or heavy tools. And no man would partner with his mother either. Although, I do not think Bastet minded much.

Inside the usual suspects were seated on their woven mats, placed in a crescent around the stone hearth. Gráinne had girls placing pillows behind her to help her stay upright on her mat. One mat for Makeda, for Bastet, and the younger girls like Lucy. I laid out my own. Only Felicia and Zoe's spots were empty. Each mat had a bowl full of blue-black-green *huitlacoche* ears to be plucked. Each of us plucked the good buds from their bowl while tossing the remains into the fire. Around us, forming the entire interior of the dome, were the twelve color specific and bejeweled stone columns, monuments to The Fountainheads; idols to those who believed.

And Bastet, with her straight back and her gray, printed plastic clothing and her imported Pacifican porcelain makeup that resisted the swelter of flames in the middle of the dome.

"Yuza, good, news?" called Gráinne directly, her smokers scrawl still strong and loud enough to overpower Bastet's nasally meandering. Her silver eyes, stoned as ever, widened as she gestured for me to sit. "Pipe, pipe, Tracy? Lucy? Somebody get Yuza the good pipe."

"Felicia showed me another infected block," I said as I brushed off a mat and plopped down.

"Girls, bring the *really good pipe*," rasped Gráinne as she took a drag from her cigarette and leaned back into her pile of pillows.

Bastet struck out, "Where is Felicia? We have not heard from her."

"I saw her at the compost on my way over. She didn't make it? I let her have a head start since she was mad at me about the infections," I said.

Makeda put down the *huitlacoche* in her hand. "Why would she be mad at you?" asked Makeda, a Pelutchian with iron blueberry skin and hard pink eyes. Pelutch, capitol of the island was up north, on the other side of Mount Tiamat. Makeda has been checking the relay stations from Pelutch down to us every three months.

"Just her tone. I didn't do nothing. What's the topic today y'all?" I asked.

Makeda held her stare on me, but said nothing. Behind her, between the crates of blank notebooks was the pink column of Jehmar, the orange column of Temar, and the green of Vladomar. I realized—

"The colors of the mushroom block infection match the colors of Fountainheads."

No one spoke except the wisps and cracking licks of the central flame. All my spirit-sisters eyes bored into me. Moths we had become, drawn to silence while some of us fluttered in place. Was I odd in that, those social emotions, of *'do this or they will exclude you'* simply do not occur for me? I kept hoping one of them would at least respond to the pattern that I'd seen.

"The radios are down across all local frequencies," said Bastet. "If you had been on time you would have known this. We already sent Kurshanabi to the mainland by boat. He should be back tonight or tomorrow."

"Jammed I bet. All the relays until this one worked fine until today. But who would want to do that?" said Makeda while looking straight at Bastet.

"And who could, while hiding the damage?" She glared between Bastet and the open flap of the dome. "I looked over the station, no obvious damage, but hafta wait for patches before I can deep dive innit. More likely the frequency is jammed up."

"From the storm? Have you seen it? Biggin looks like," I said.

Bastet snapped off, "if the storm was raining down on us then perhaps Yuza, but no, that would not knock out our radio transmitter."

"Who knows?" I asked.

"Anyone who has tried to use their radio today. *Really?* Yuza don't you ever think before you speak?" asked Bastet.

I'd brushed her off as I usually had to, but seeing her boy out there in the muck added a bit of fire to my lips. "Maybe ask your boy? He is always tinkering with things when no is looking."

"Yuza!" bellowed Gráinne. "Dammit, Lucy, where is the pipe!?"

"Aye, palanda doovremisosio," I said to Gráinne. Then to Bastet, "I apologize to you Bastet. I should not have risen your boys name." Bastet looked past me.

Lucy, Gráinne's Amraken hospice nurse, returned with the *really good pipe: an* orange coral steamroller. "Come on, come on now girls. Ain't time for pulling hairs."

Makeda stood, "I gotta get back to my babes y'all and without phone or radio there's no way for me to tell the babysitter I'll be late. If y'all would just modernize this'd be a stupid simple fix."

Bastet cleared her throat, "You are correct Makeda. This situation proves our single point of failure, as I have spoken of before—"

"Peace! I want to hear no more of anything but PEACE!" said Gráinne.

Lucy held the peace pipe before Bastet. She faked taking a puff. Then Lucy brought the pipe to me and I took my prescribed peace with glee. Gráinne's next toke put her to sleep.

"How are your journals coming along?" Bastet asked us. I flipped all the bent blank pages at her. Bastet rolled her eyes at me and pulled her own mostly filled notebook out and down onto her mat. "Makeda?"

"We handle our own data just fine little miss quisling," said Makeda as she walked away.

Bastet returned her attention to me, "Yuza, without computers so much of the community's history and culture will be lost forever. The least you can do is write things down. Daily journal writing is a scientifically proven therapeutic for all forms of stress. Is there any other issues I should know about? Your son Yal also has not turned in a single notebook yet. Most Amraken boys would have long social media records, full of photos with their friends, sport victories, girlfriends, all sorts of things. All lost due to a preference to do more work? I don't understand you."

"Lucy, Lucy, the pipe. Please, oh, thank you. THANK YOU," after a toke I asked, "What?" Bastet turned red from that haha!

"My boy is the only mistake Akachi did not make with us Moths. You are the oldest of us and yet you are the youngest of us in spirit Yuza. You simply will not last in what is to come," said Bastet. *(Maybe a* little wonky since its hard to remember exactly how she told me she hates me while I was stoned.)

"Baizan! Get over yourself Bastet. Come work with us in the vineyards sometime, get the stress out. Catch a real moth, let it go, smell some flowers, feel tiny with us underneath Sabaoth's rays."

Shouts, boys, metal clanging from back near the open flap entrance broke our chatter.

Spryaig, slides, face first across the linoleum floor of the dome. My Yalson steps into the dome and puts his foot on Spryaig's back. Several other teen boys are lined up back outside the entrance.

"Forgive me for smearing him across the floor Yuzama, Gráinne, Bastet and Makeda. Forgive me thrice Lucy," he actually bowed his head at her, but Lucy focused on holding and lighting the pipe. Without any words. I wondered if she was deaf.

Yal held up the steel bolt wrapped with copper wire Spryaig had been toying with. "As Akachi says, 'when comms go down, look for who can, and for who would' and here he is."

Before any of us could say another word. A motor engine, not one, or two, but many with rumbling engines grew louder and louder. I leaned near the fire to look up through the smokestack. Airplanes were dropping something which whistled before crooning into a thousand million screams. Yal rallied the boys outside to break into the transmission station and force Spryaig to repair what he had damaged. But none of it mattered once the bombs started falling. These armoring bodies cannot see or hear the VaporFlame. They madden, their faces redden. My sisters all shriek. What are we to do against such violence? The sea burned with blue fire. The vapor mixed with other smoke and stole the sky from us. And we forgot to question how the spores of the varicolored mycelium might be spreading while we were all trying to survive.

Aktaly Moth, that will be the name of my Daughter. No matter the man, that will be her name.

To honor the stigmatized mother of man: Akamoth. Sacred daughter, like Iris the rainbow herself. And Eurydice the patron of every offered and dowry laden gown, who've been written out of their own stories. No matter the man, the name of my daughter will be Aktaly Moth.

Dear Aktaly, I must consider myself cursed and blessed for being Yal's Mother during this Elengen Twilight. Broken, violet–red sun rays splintered the blackened storm cloud sky. The wind told us to remain, it was a heavy, sodden tumult, but us being human, just had to do something other than wait. The boys had their weapons, tools and packs from the training *koryos*. Yal, being oldest and blooded had become their chief. He will be the last I fear, at least until Akachi returns one day.

Most of the activity remained in the north. From the *Taradome* we could see the green lightning flashing in the clouds just above the mountains. Only one airship landed around Tia-Tara. A handful of Soldiers, five or so, began going from house to house while their red, crablike airship hovered silently above. Wilting any trees it came close to.

With minutes to decide, Yal did his best. And all I could do was watch. I would speak and no sound would come out. I remember though, what perhaps no one else will.

Yal put iron shackles around Spryaig's neck and hands, with chains riding up between his groin. His gangly frame had no chance of escape or defense against my Yal— taller than all present, shoulders and neck thicker than all present, his crimson eyes glowing more than any present. "We are betrayed! The runt and these quislings," he points his obsidian knife at Bastet, who was not yet chained, but eager boys did have more shackles on standby. How quickly tools become weapons, those shackles were meant for big cats! Not people, not our own people, not *for my own sister*. And yet, we had been betrayed perhaps. And for no clear reason. Or, were we all jumping to conclusions? Maybe Bastet had nothing to do with this? I tried to catch her eyes but she trembled and curled up into herself. As if she had not expected this could ever happen to her.

And my Yalson, the best of Akachi's Amraken–Elengen brood, was my own blood. For all the dangers around us. I stood behind my Yalson, neither sun nor sweat would mar his skin, like unrefined iron, flecked with sun-stone freckles. He stood in front of me as the spitting image of his Father, of Akachi.

"Half of you will guard the Taradome. You will force the truth from the traitors lips. The rest will meet these *Slobes* as they try to take our homes. Do not face any alone. It is they who must climb our muddy hills. Hit and run, avoid face to face if they have rifles or worse. Let them climb and become heavy. Makeda, where is your truck? Can it reach the north?" said Yal.

The boys shifted their packs around and passed gear between those who would stay and those who would travel. Spryaig and Bastet, were shackled to the Taradome before anyone departed. Gráinne remained asleep back inside. *What could I have done better?* This all happened so fast. And I was still a little stoned. My attention kept veering to the Amraken airship as it crept up Tia-Tara.

"M'truck's on the north crest of Tara, past Yuzasis place, right on the way," said Makeda. "If they only got one ship down 'ere we can zap it down. Got an EM rifle onboard an all. Seats five."

"That's it!" Yal raised his voice to a commanding volume. "Tradition has us hunt big cats: lions, tigers, scaled lynxes. Well as of today we are changing our prey. Men have come to take our blood and our homes and our future. We shall take theirs instead. Their blood will make you Manticore! This is Akachi's way!"

All the boys joined Yal in his chant of his Father's words:

"Kill the stronger heart with the weaker steel. Become exhausted, starve, banish sleep from your body, become flesh, nerve and bone and make the Lion's flesh your own! Purge the boy! Make the Man! Be brazen, yours is no disgrace! Become Manticore!"

I followed Yal and a dozen armed boys back the way I'd come from the Axon hillock. The street sweep broom was laying upright against the stone retainer wall along the paved path. *Had that man gotten away? Wait, I didn't know who that was, could he have been involved with this? Was Spryaig innocent? How did the man know our language?*

Oh, just more and more useless questions I'll never get answered. The boys had only air rifles. They caught one soldier, covered in green armor, who was fighting the mud after breaking through a neighbor's iron gate. They peppered him until he twisted and fell over, face first into the mud. Yal scooped up the Soldier's long black rifle. My heart stopped for a few beats as Yal held the rifle against the back of the Soldier's helmet, where the skin was and I must make my peace now or I never will. Yal was protecting me, us, Elengen.

We trekked through the finer estates who had l kaliche yards and lovely terraces and fountains which we used to bypass the main muddy stairwell. Gunshots would ring out in the distance every few minutes.

Our group dwindled as the boy split off to other homes. At the fence of our home we waited as the airship wilted my gardens, herbs, tomatoes, a quarter acre of corn. The water in our fishpond evaporated. Three of the soldiers were talking to each other—right in my own front yard! *Baizan!* Yal lined up the rifle, but did not shoot. He did not blink until two of the Soldiers were pulled back up into the airship. Once alone Yal leaped into action and three boys followed him.

The Soldier's whole body was covered in green armor with five black insect eyes. Yal fired every bullet he had at the Soldier. Holes were torn through my rose bushes and the windows and walls of our home. The Soldier simply stood there. The shots stopped and all the boys attacked with whatever they had. They did their best, but the Soldier simply stood there, safe in his armor. One by one the boys had to stop their futile assault. Their hands were bloody from flesh striking metal. No matter how much they wanted to hurt this Soldier they simply could not. Yal persisted, the boys tried chains, but their combined strength could do nothing against the weight of the Soldier.

Today, the boys would would remain boys.

This soldier, armed and armored made one twisting move to disarm him, then take the knife and snapped it into pieces. He pushed Yal to the ground and held him firm until he stopped stirring. Then, and with all the gods that have ever been as my witness—this Soldier removed his helmet before us, stepped back and knelt. His hair and face were like ours. And his face had the grief we'd not yet had the pause to realize. He listened to Yal curse him.

"Its not your fault," said the Soldier. *"I am sorry. I don't expect you to forgive me. This ain't the mission I thought it was."*

Yal calmed, seeing this Man, this Soldier who was not like the others. Lynx, Corporal Michael Lynx. *This* man, he struggled between his own wavering jowls to hold his composure.

He said one more thing, "I'll tell my Sergeant this place is clear."

Lynx, left us with some monies, the green Amraken papers. Because of him I have my home. Because of him I have my Boy. Because of him I have my garden where death can still compost where life can still grow.

Yal and his boys are silent, defeated, no, they are who they are, just boys, who tried to be men and were put in their place. Akachi would punish them, but because Akachi was not here to lead them would he punish himself for letting his home, his wives, his brood to be threatened so? No, there would be skins, drying in the wind, and skulls on spits. Or am I confusing Akachi the Man with Akachi the Legend? No, if Akachi had been here I think we would have been worse off.

Makeda made no comment about their manhood. She saw what I saw. We were blessed and cursed for Cpl. Lynx to be the one to stand and not need to fight. Who knows what would have happened if it'd been any other kind of man?

"I can't wait for anything Yuza. This was supposed to be a day trip, Dio and Zani need me. There's no tellin' what they babysitter might do once they feel the first explosions." She left with two of the boys. I saw her climb into her truck on the other side of Axon hillock. They drove away in peace. The airship did begin to hover in their direction but it did not follow.

Even if a bit ionized. None of this should be. I know I must be grateful. The Lynx asked for nothing, unlike most soldiers who arrived each day from the north as if Tiamat had a few late bloomers.

3/27/1991

Dear Aktaly, Felicia found her way back to our home. I asked her for all that she knew and had seen, which was nothing more than I knew or had seen.

We embraced for moments enough to find the last scents of our old lives within the tangle of each others unwashed hair. Oh Felicia! We Moths continue! Sweet, humble Felicia right on the cusp of adulthood. Always the arbiter between Bastet and I. And she who'd sought the eye of Yal.

"And Bastet? What of her boy?" I asked.

"I don't know. I've not seen her."

"I think Bastet betrayed us all," I concluded.

"We don't know that. We don't know anything! She might be dead. She might be behind it. She might be captured she—"

"Hey! Hey! No, we can't spiral Felicia. Not now," I hugged her and held her until her tears passed. Yal came into the room and Felicia forgot herself to tend to him, but he shrugged her off. Ignorant boy. Yal tried our walkies-talkies and house radio but they were still distorted with the same sound looping. It hurt our ears so we would not try it more than once every few hours. Felicia and I nurse Yal's cuts bruises with wild lettuce ointment. We eat oranges and I place the peel over my boy's eyes as I hold him, his body is bigger than mine; I hold my Son and we weep together for all that we will never have. Then I called Felicia in. She'd combed her hair and washed her face and her feet and put on some of my old clothes. I lent her some of my turquoise bangles.

"You fought the Soldiers?" she asked him.

Yal shrugged off his wounds and pulled her close, "Lemme tell you…"

I left the room to let Felicia and Yal be together. Here's to hoping.

Dear Aktaly, they've got us every which way they can without putting their hands on us. How long can this last? I have to assume these Soldiers are not members of an Amraken Peace Corp NGO.

Gráinne is staying with Yalson and I. She is not speaking and only sitting in the glass sun room, soaking up solar rays. I keep her fed and hydrated. Her silence makes everything else hard to hear.

Writing under lock down is all I have right now, other than tending the remains of my tomatoes and flower beds of course. Most is compost. Yal keeps finding sticks to sharpen. He doesn't know what else to do but figure out some way to fight. But this is no enemy to be fought with sticks and stones. Especially since, despite all the weapons these Amrakens brought, most seemed aimed at the Earth, not at any of us. Engines echoes through the hillocks and the dust will not leave the air. I think I'm intellectualizing again, and, well, this might be the kind of time where that would be best. Maybe that's what happened to Gráinne. Maybe she is feeling what I am not.

I remember in the Amraken school, mentions of the French, Belgian, Spanish, British and Chinese, of how they'd invade a land with pieces of paper by getting the land owners to sell their titles away. How they would select some members, usually a minority of some kind and give them privileges over the majority. By hook or by crook whole nations were renamed overnight and whole new countries and borders emerged from the end of a thick red pen. *Did Bastet make a deal? Did she know? Was someone else to blame entirely?*

These Soldiers with their metal hearts and bodies see themselves as masters of Akachi's land, Glia's sea and Sabaoth's sky. They cannot see the interconnections of what they break with their boots. All within the Unkenoma shape and have been shaped through Tia-Sophia's webs of cause and effect. No individual holds ultimate significance over the whole. We are integral to the unfolding music of this universe. Whose song began before anyone had a voice to sing with. Myriads, radiate from Sabaoth, Holy Lord, to the phytoplankton of the deepest sea.

I must find a way to connect these people and the island. Providing purpose, providing meaning through our role in Her-story, not His-story. We are more than our biological legacy. Imagine if we could stimulate our curiosity, creatively to contribute to the work-in-progress story of this conscious symphony. I can keep a clear head and not panic. We will protest this. We have no weapons but our voices, our words, and our wills. If we don't use them, we deserve what comes.

3/31/1991

Excerpt from the Old-Babylon Times:

Anti-conscription protests are popping up all over Elengen, even in areas seen as generally supportive of Amraken's war effort against Vlaruska. This comes as the Amraken government has been teasing a major mobilization, as the military is in dire need of thousands of military age males.

The new military draft is already approved by executive order to reduce the age limit of selective service conscription from 27 to 15. While also increasing the penalties for those failing to register. The Old-Babylon Times has reported, "The Amraken military is facing an existential shortage of cybernetic-infantry nodes, leading to exhaustion and diminished morale on the front line."

From radio feeds across the front line, soldiers and commanders declared that personnel deficits were their most critical problem now, as Vlaruska has regained the offensive initiative on the Pelutch front. The Vlaruskan forces are stepping up their hypersonic attacks,' the report continued.

In a rarity, The Old-Babylon Times on Sunday, detailed a protest that popped up over the weekend. Villages in the south have been a primary source of soldiers for the Amraken Army.

The roadblock took place on Tuesday along the hillock of the Tia-Tara region. This allegedly began with unfounded rumors in local women's groups that draft officials were coming to find the village's remaining men, the Military Police said in a statement. About a hundred women blocked a road, and the protest turned violent when the Soldiers mistook a woman for a man.

The woman, Yuza Moth, whose anecdotal quotes could not be fact checked into a *Scatterweb* post, was said to have said, that the source of the anxiety was the military recruitment system.

The Times observes, "The plans for calling up more soldiers to fight in fifth generation warfare was something nobody should worry about. Troops are still fighting from the very start of the war who have, in an extremely compelling amount of cases expressed gratitude at having done their duty, and have it extended past their military service end date. They get five times overtime with a raise for every month they survive! Most fight with keyboards, except the Manticore Units..."

Dear Aktaly, our protest worked. The Soldiers have backed off for now. Of course they will return, but our protest can be an example for others. Peace, non-violence, clear, articulation of grievances. Despite what our actions might end up being spun into, we stood our ground and made ourselves heard. All people on Elengen left the tri-super state world to live where we live. Men and Women and all other forms of Human Being deserve the right to bodily autonomy. To conscript someone is only just above direct bodily torture for the lowest of the low that an authority can coerce an individual to resort to. Especially when it's a foreign power seeking bodies to contend with its own population.

Our protest stopped those who were left, like my Yalson, from being taken though. I really must wonder what these Amrakens think they are doing here? They beach their ships, unload their construction machines, and begin devouring our island, our home. Then they steal, not us, not the woman as per usual invaders, no, these people seem driven by some deeper desperation. Almost...no, how could a fleet of military ships with all their technology be running from something? Former fields have been leveled into smooth gray plains with cables and pipes forming the skeletons of buildings their machines fill in with concrete. Our local agriculture of corn, plantain, coconut, olive, and citrus, and all of our herbs have been purged. They seemed to not understand any of the other plants, all of our tubers and garlic and lettuces were untouched. I can't make sense of their actions. There may not have been a plan at all for us in their extractivist scenarios.

And, strangest of all, some of the Soldiers actually turned coat and stood beside us against their own kind. Michael was one of them. There has to be consequences for that. Don't they have a chain of leaders, or direction or something? A hierarchy, they certainly must. But, maybe in the minds of those who protested conscription with us, they were also questioning their own leadership alongside what crimes had already been committed.

This must be exceptionally hard for anyone who hasn't had any education on social engineering. Without this perspective of mine, without my internal voice of reason, all of this would feel like a demonic invasion to devour our entire way of life. I think if the Amrakens would at least tell us what they're really here for, it would clear a lot of things up. Starting with why there is still no radio communications for anyone.

04/02/1991

A television
exists.
It only stops
when I turn it off.
Yal loves it though
more I fear
than me.
For hours he watches Soldiers
the same kind as
those who resemble his father
burn those who resemble his father
obliterate those who resemble his father
chain and collar those who resemble his father.
And when I cut the cable of the demonic device:
Yal,
my boy
my one and only
roared at me;
Like a leonine manticore.
The Army has taken my boy.
Said, he has potential.
Said, he will be a hero.
Said, he will be safe.
Now I am alone.
With a new television,
complements of the Army
Searching
through the vaporous screen.
Wondering,
which boy is which
which pain is which.

Part 2: The Cradle

From The People of Pelutch by Hed Remar

Amraken encompasses the entirety of the western hemisphere. In 1492 CE the Spanish Reconquista failed and the Iberian monarchies were culled. The Iberian Peninsula remained a diverse, multi-cultural region, with a continued coexistence and intermixing of Abrahamic populations. The Portuguese and Spanish remained focused within the European sphere, lacking major naval capabilities and resource-driven ambition.

The Aztec, advanced to the north, met the Mazatec, Pueblo, and Apache peoples and formed an alliance of non-aggression and equitable trade. A surprising arrival of Chinese and Indian sailors accelerated technological progress of metallurgy and agriculture. The Comanche— after coming in fourth place during a annual cook off —sought to disrupt the alliance. And the region remained divided ever since, among who makes the best beans and barbacoa. When Portuguese sailors arrived in 1519, the Aztec already had magazine fed repeating crossbows and body armor for themselves and their horses from their fierce feuds with the Comanche. Peace was an easy choice for both sides at that time.

The Amraken progressed through their own civil wars during the 18th and 19th centuries. Since 1865 they have slowly been spreading their version of democracy to the west coast of Afrasenkin and the eastern edges of Pacifica. Amraken defeated Vlaruska in the 1984 War for Polaris, also known as the War for the Arctic Ring, but that Army never returned to the global south as far as anyone knows.

Amraken has been the sole military power across the globe since then. Strange that the largest army ever assembled seemed to always need another war to fight. You'd think if they were so great at fighting, that we'd have world peace by now.

As always, cui bono?

4/03/1991

Dear Aktaly, the Moths have been barred from Tia-Tara entirely by the Amraken Soldiers. All who fought with whatever weapons they had were no match for the surprise attack here in the south. Perhaps up north Makeda was faring better in Pelutch with the airfields and military base.

I have an apartment on the third floor of a small building. It has electric, metal doors that groan when they close. The abominate thing is made of rough concrete lines spat out in layers.

These people can fly and carry mountains of metal through the clouds. They cover the farmland with solar orchid arrays and fields and fields of construction sites. They demolish our hatcheries for turbines. The rivers and streams have been dammed. The wells located and plugged. We have faucets, bittersweet with hints of lithium zinc. A fridge of white food boxes that read 'Codex A'

Michael, tried to argue against his fellow soldiers again as they returned with airships to snatch whoever they wished from the sky with hooked ropes. But he was just one man and his own kind pinned him into the ground.

There was no time—I had to say something to my Yalson. Because he ran out into the yard when the airship came over our home. He cried out, "Here I am! Here I am!" with his sharpened sticks in his hands. Felicia was frozen, mouth agape, hair tousled, and half-dressed watching him bolt out into the yard, right through the garden beds. With moments I sprinted for him, and pulled his eyes to look right into mine. I told him to learn their culture, their language, their slang and how to talk and think like them so that he can survive among them. "*You have to give them a reason to want you alive.*"

Horrible, horrible things I said. That is how it went. *Horrible.* My words will linger on his soul for the rest of his years. *Oh Yal.* He has been sent right out of his youth and into the horrible realities of just how bad life can be. If he cannot read, speak, write or think well, then he will become just another warm body for someone to put to work. I hope he figures out the best of what I meant.

We'd been gathered up into trucks and brought to this walled in village barely a kilometer from our own still standing homes back on Tia-Tara. Our farms have been walled off. Locks have been put on the doors of the wood mill and the community kitchen and Charybdis, our waterwheel hydro-electric station.

Where is my heart? All of us we've been ransacked and yet none of us cry? What has been done to us? Many of us, like Gráinne remain silent and skeletal, her frailty uncanny. She sits around an electric heater. She still has girls helping her, and making sure she eats and drinks.

The Television down the hall in the front room turned itself on. *"Yuza...Yuza,"* it whispered. I checked and the voice was not Gráinne.

I sat next to her, silent as she was and talked. I told her all the words I could not write. A gentle caress of her frail hand was all she had to give me.

I was the oldest. Felicia looked to me. Bastet always wanted to outdo me. Zoe abandoned us.

An Amraken was thrown in here with us. Michael Lynx, the same who'd stood alongside me in our protest against the Amrakens. He had nothing on him but his clothes. He wandered around the quarter catching glares from everyone.

He had helped me. He was alone. Maybe he could help me find Yal.

I went to him. We shared an apple. He showed me how to interact with the PX building next to our apartments. He tells me since I'se born Amraken I'm automatically a citizen again. He tells me I will be able to have my own monies and will be able to sign my own papers. I ask why I would not be able to do so otherwise and he tried to explain what digital ID is and how its tied to allowing the use of money.

New Amraken, same as the old Amraken.

04/07/1991

I look at my plastic card with my face, frozen within it.
I reach for myself, to get my face back.
Part of me I cannot retrieve.
Part of me is in their plastic now.
Part of me has become plastic now.
Part of me is not alive.
Yuza Moth, I shall always be.
On their plastics
printed beige
the yellow of my morning offerings
and their papers
and discs
and tapes
and drives
and sticks
and crystals
I have become 2141969555 Teal Yuza Moth number 01.
We needed no walls between a world that moves with
the wind and a world that is still composting,
unsure if it'll be sand, dirt, clay or electricity.
That builds the New Ma
Yuza, Nu Me.

06/20/1991

Dear Aktaly, this is your creation story. Michael and I were automatically married due to our increasing associations, according to an Amraken policy of domestic partnerships that their computer algorithms call laws. We had no ceremony, no pictures exist, only a paper reminder that we were now in a new tax bracket. And that Michael was no longer allowed in the barracks and could no longer ask the Army for assistance any longer. He has been, how did he say, *dishonorably discharged for the crime of insubordination* for his role in our protest.

I suppose having a conscience is at odds with being the foot soldier of an Empire. Michael is a human being, Elengen welcomes him, he has bled for our blood. If that sounds like a metaphor, I do not know of all that he has lost. He does not speak of his heart. His light brown skin, stretches along his square jaw and he turns ruddy instead of red. He asks for my help with his papers, taxes, resumes, deployment histories, prescriptions, assets, all the tentacles of Amraken bureaucracy we of Elengen had sought to escape.

I put my hands on his and said, "what comes first Michael. You, your papers, or all these numbers about you?"

His brow scrunched, his dimples showed contempt. I do not react, and meet his response with a true smile of my eyes. "Whaddya mean?" he asked.

I rubbed my own long, calloused fingers through his leathery fingers. "Say you get all your papers in order as you feel they need to be. Today, tomorrow, what do those do for you? I am not new to bureaucracy. Someone will find them in their mailbox and filter them in a database. And your life story will sit there. Your pain, your worries, your hopes will sit there in that mailbox until some clerk opens it up and runs it through another filter. They will not even read it. Meanwhile, what will you be doing? *Waiting?* We need food."

Michael did not pull away. His brow, jaw, his whole face quivers then softens. Those teal eyes of his—oh Aktaly—I saw the boy within him. That boy who long ago had papers plied to his face, his arms, how papers had enveloped him. I knew because I saw my own father in him then, and my brothers and my grandfathers. I am from his world, all on Elengen came from Amraken. We all knew the cost of white sugar, asbestos, high fructose corn syrup, seed oils, aluminum, formaldehyde, lead, DDT, fluoride, glyphosate and bisephenol-a. We remember the drunken spittle coming not just from men, but from anyone who poisons themselves in any circumstance no matter their rationalizations. And we remember the methane and ammonia of our landfills and septic pools. We knew an entire civilization, who forgot that the map is not the territory. Plato's Cave is made of LED, Wi-fi and RGB. There is a reason cybernetics, eugenics and public relations developed together. Without another word from me, right then and there Michael woke up! And I knew that he would be your Father Aktaly.

"Shit. You're fucking right!" He leaped from his plastic chair and spins around, slowly, inspecting all that remained of both our lives: clothes, papers, plastic containers wrapped in plastic and containing a dozen white boxes labeled Codex A, *also* wrapped in plastic. Oh, and a single, used microwave with tape holding the swing door shut.

He ripped one open. Dense tan bricks plopped. He picked one up, brushed it off and tried to take a bite. He winced; the block remained unbroken. He read the instruction on the flap. Then he tossed it down and ripped through eleven more.

"This is all dehydrated microwave bullshit. Worse than field rations! What the fuck?"

"Whatever shall we feast upon my newly anointed Husband?"

That confused him again and, once more this man surprised me. He went straight for one particular paper. The notice of our *domestication*. At that he smirked. "Those motherfuckers goddamn. Well Yuza, its looking like we needa start acting like a team." He looked at the paper again. *"Goddamn."*

"Yes," was all I said since he came to the conclusion we both needed him to come to. Perhaps this was the true reason for his discharge from their Army. Michael had the Vaporflame within him. He was no animal, fleeting from reaction to reaction. Michael had a brain and a heart. He could think and change his mind on a dime. He was the Man I needed in the world his kind had wrought. I pulled a sachet of seeds from the folds of my clothes. Where, even the probing hands of the Peace Officers had not found every pocket and personal store.

"Growth will take time, but with this we can grow our own food. Vladomar will hear us once we plant the first seed."

"Vlado?"

"Vladomar is the Fountainhead of Growth," I did not want to opine.

"Wait, I remember a briefing before we landed. About Quantum AI defenses, but that's the north."

I leaned up against him. He was not much taller than me. I made sure he felt my warmth around his arms and upon his chest. "We need to forage and scout and plant. Or our own hunger will lure us into their microwaved traps Michael. You are smart. You will learn as we go. I do not need to explain everything."

"I'm smart? You're the smart one! I'm following you. Where we going?"

I had more sachets but did not reveal them. I gathered some of the hard plastic from the packages. I figured it enough for a basic trowel. Michael emptied all of the bags he could. We set out to plant the seeds needed for the hope of food security.

Outside thick gray clouds swirled like three snakes above the Organo Mountains to the north, past the teal and yellow flowers of the otherwise muddy shrub of the Tia-Tara hillock.

Our apartment building was hastily built on the southern bank of the Tio-Tatanka river, which ran between us and Tia-Tara. Yellow dumpsters were lined up along the left side of the lot. Past those an alleyway stretched between more of these printed concrete buildings. I craned my neck to gauge their height. *How could they build such things so fast?* I mean, sure, I can imagine them pouring concrete out of some machine and calling it a day, but every single window had a metal cage holding the air conditioners in. Machines are never so meticulous; only people when they perform as if they were machines.

"Michael, were these already built before—" I still haven't found the right word to refer to that first day. Also, I still have not felt that initial day. If I hadn't written the before and after down I probably would've suppressed that as well. I think the Amrakens wrote their own story plenty in all the craters and the sores they have left us with.

I asked Michael about his view of the invasion. I reminded myself, that Michael did not raise a hand against us when he could have. He stood against his own kind for us. I find myself trusting him. And I listened because his words are his honest response.

"Yeah, prolly, I don't know Yuza. I didn't know nothin' comin' out here you know? I didn't think about what I was doing all the time. Orders, of course that's we always say. That's what we're all trained to say, to not think. *That's an Order!*"

He is talking plain. He wears the shame of his ignorance for his role in his crimes. I keep asking and listening. He will help me begin to understand what all of this has been for.

Michael and I explored the quarter. A few dozen Elengen were packed like us into these apartments. The street running through the quarter was full of electric bicycles and humming scooters driven by Amrakens wearing floral, summer clothes and shimmering with various plastic white accessories.

I pointed at the glowing violet lines around my sandals embedded within the sidewalk and street. The day was dim. Perhaps my eyes were tired. The colors segued from contact with the asphalt.

"Smart streets. Here check it—" Michael took a step and lines around his feet turned teal. "Some stupid shit from back home. Matches to eye colors. Shits expensive, prolly had some excess and sold it to our crews in bulk for cheap." As the words left his mouth, his face twisted for a second before he sighed, "what a shit show man," to one thought, and "they didn't give us a map or tell us about the territory," to another thought. Fascinating how he does that on the fly and consistently.

Across from us: a translucent glass world of offices, shops and service centers, compacted into blocks surrounded by razor wire. Soldiers posted at the only entrance right in the intersection itself. Michael explored the two paths down the street where there were parking lots, and strip malls still under construction. Both ended with army checkpoints where only the Amrakens were passing through gleefully on their silent electric bikes.

There was some brief patches of loose earth where whole trees had been uprooted. Even those had red lines marked future construction sites. To my right, towering over the entire quarter was a holographic billboard with the word FORGIVE looping in a dripping green motion which morphed into the word ZOE.

Why would a sign above an internment zone ask us to forgive life? It could not be my sister. How many girls in the world, or this island are named Zoe? No, it does not mean its her.

Airships, and gleaming crescents above us strafed through green, blinding beams. I could only shoot my gaze from one senseless aberration to the next. The metal birds landed around us and in the street. Some people crashed and others would laugh at them while holding their rectangles out in front, recording perhaps? How can they be so callous?

These birds had leaves or flowers in place as any natural bird would have feathers. Otherwise they were all metal, dull on the back with chrome on the belly. Black beaks, with serrated indigo lines that matched their beady red eyes. Patrolling Soldiers flicked galvanized bolts at the birds to draw them away from the bicyclists. An Army truck with a half-moon antenna pulled out from the checkpoint in the intersection. I didn't hear it do anything, but all the birds looked at the truck, *shrieked*, then flew away. Back beyond their walls and toward Tia-Tara.

"Michael this—*I cannot.*"

His worry matched mine. He offered his hand and led us around the rest of the lot back through the ground floor of the apartment building. He'd push past other Soldiers with their new wives and various mothers with their daughters. He'd open doors, apologize and ask for where the courtyard, or rest area, or green space or anything like that might be.

Eventually we crossed to the other side of the apartment building. Despite the lingering haze above us, Sabaoth still shone bright as any summer day. A fence twice Michael's height blocked us from going further. We found what we needed though.

There was black soil patches and green, weedy, blankets of grass. A small pool had formed in the moistened tread tracks likely left behind by the Amraken engineers. And, there was a bench, oddly enough, with panels carved of wood, rough, as if by hand, despite still being wrought iron and bolted to the ground. Someone else had been through here and had preserved this newly sacred land.

"Fellas went nuts huh? All this mess. Geez. Wanna sit? You think this waters any good?" I sat down. He sniffed the pond. "Smells pungent and metallic, waddya think?" He craned his neck toward the sky. "Not enough direct sunlight to purify. Sitches tough Yuza. Ain't a whole lot we can do."

My eyes, my blood, the feelings I had not yet felt became vertigo. I snapped my eyes shut before the nausea could begin.

Once again I rejected myself. *Think. Think. Think. Think. Think Yuza what to do where to go who to speak to, to barter with, to haggle, negotiate. That is how we survive. We fawn, we do not run, we cannot fight, to freeze is to die so we must fawn. Something has to give, not everything, but something that I will always be grateful and regretful forever for. It's that or I will never get to meet you Aktaly. For you my future child. Yes, for you, as Akamoth would do.*

I did not have to speak. I gathered what stones there were, gave the larger to Michael and he followed my lead as we dug three furrows. The black soil was perfect, rough, filled with worms, and rich

as the best raw earth could be. I gave him each seed
to plant. He planted them as I told him. He covered
the seeds, gently, as I instructed him. We cupped
water in our bare hands from the small pond into the
furrows. His larger hand held more water and my
small hands were underneath his to catch any leaks I
could. We planted corn, tomatoes, peppers, onions,
garlic, radish, ginger, turmeric, lavender, oregano,
sunflowers and daffodils. And every seed had
dormant spores of *Reishi*.

The wind kept us cool through our humbling
task. And our efforts did not go unnoticed. Children,
girls, a whole giggling gang of them had burst into
our quiet, sweltering work. Elengen girls, not
Amraken, they recognized what Michael and I were
doing. I did not need to ask. Without mind of dirt or
sweat, all of them joined us in the planting. We
would not have been able to complete the day
without them. Felicia showed up while she was
searching for the girls.

"Yuza, a garden! Awesome. *But who is this?*" she
asked while pointing at Michael, covered in dust and
muddy sweat. I took a break from our labors.

"This is Michael. He is a good man."

"Michael?"

"Howdy," Michael brushed dirt off on his jeans
and offered her a handshake.

She looked him over and took a step back, "Sure,
okay, but why's an Amraken over here?"

"He helped me. Remember the protest? He joined us then and was punished for it," I said.

Felicia's big brown eyes lit up, "Oooh." She turned to Michael, "Floyd says he misses drinking with you."

"Fuck him and his bullshit insubordination charges. Tell him to have fun babysittin' the engineers on his own," said Michael.

Felicia grimaced, then shook her head and called for the girls to come along. "Make sure to get your phone setup before tomorrow," she said while flicking on a flashlight from her watch. The day was done, a coral twilight was puttering away. I'se might grateful she could light our way back into the building and to the stairs. Amraken particularity proved itself—only half the light bulbs worked.

"My what?" I asked her while squinting from the white LED cone slashing away at the darkness and turning the ten or so of us into spider like shadows stretching across the floor and up every wall.

"The watch, its smartie or something, connected to the phone. That's what they call it Yuza. I don't know what it is okay."

"Its for ID, smartphones and bio-metrics. We use 'em for everything nowadays. I didn't think about it at first. But yeah, we prolly got some sitting in some stupid hard to open box back up top there," said Michael. His upward pointing gestures became a serpentine shadow that reached the ceiling.

Once we reached the second floor of the building I saw what she meant. Women stood in the hall outside their apartment doors with their daughters. Each held a small rectangle, their 'phone', in their hands, colored, and matched to a watch on their left hands and a necklace. All matching, all sequenced. Michael and I had neither. He recognized this, thanked Felicia for pointing this out, then he led me back into our unit, our appointed abode. Our cell.

All the androgynous Amraken couriers, in uniforms of brown polos with matching shorts and fuzzy yellow socks. Most were carrying steaming brown bags of food and white pizza boxes. The receiver would tap their 'phone' against the delivery persons 'phone' before abruptly turning away, without either looking each other in the eye.

Back in our basically bare apartment I watched Michael search and search through all of our packaging for our phones, watches and collars. One phone, for me, labeled with my ID, and a watch, but the collar was for him—*to place upon me.*

And this Man, in an instant saved me from the terror that all my Elengen sisters had faced before me. Michael ripped the collar apart, despite its bronze tendrils expanding into a writhing metal hydra. And he struggled with it all anew. That is what I responded to, helping aid a moral man fight a monster trying to claim us both in different ways.

Both of our bodies were stabbed, pronged, gashed by the bronze hydra. The Amraken garbage disposal was sharp enough to do what our bare hands could not.

"I'm done, just fucking done Michael. Plug in the goddamned microwave, lets eat and go to sleep."

He did as a good man would. We ate in humid silence as we cooled off in front of the window air conditioner. I began a hot shower. I didn't think about only having a bar of soap. I called to Michael.

"What do you need?" he asked.

"Help me summon my daughter," I said.

And that is how you came to be.

Dear, Aktaly.

06/21/1991

A man, a woman, waylaid on bearskins.
Draw the leaves and bees and flowers of the trees
they perceive in each other's eyes.
Four forests: the one that is, that is not, that
could be and will never be.
What is the line of discernment?
Without discernment, can either side be seen?
The young life looks at the old life.
Smooth or creased knuckles, upright or bent
spines, hairline a few inches this way or that.
Wrinkles, folds, graying and creaking bodies.
The eyes though,
cannot hide the similitude of experience
of every frozen and evolving ego.

08/04/1991

Dear Aktaly, for the past month, Michael and I have been focused on building up the garden. This included showing Felicia how to teach the rest of the girls to check for weeds to cull and healthy shoots to transplant. She knew what to do, but I had to explain to her that she had to learn how to teach as its own skill. Being competent around novices is not enough to make them equally competent, especially with children. Once she thought of herself at the same age she was able to understand.

"Is that how you learned?" she asked me.

I told her, "this is how the all the world moves, through the soil that other hands have tended."

That's all in my Garden Journal though. I wasn't sure about including it with this personal journal.

Makeda Nysos returned today with her two year old son Dio and infant daughter Zani. She had to hike the entire way on foot. Luckily she wasn't by herself, she actually brought several dozen people with her. All from Pelutch, and mostly men. Despite all those been wounded fighting the Amrakens in the north. They had crossed the Tio-Tatanka while still in the mountains. I am proud of my spirit-sister for what she has done. She made it back home, she found her children, she led survivors to safety and she lives to tell me all this herself, with her babies on her back no less.

Michael was wary at first as the Pelutchians filled in around the apartment building. Some actually approached from the rear and climbed over the back fence. Others through the eastern checkpoint. They had rifles which *'zap zipped'* and made electric things pop.

Michael, Felicia and I had been in the back garden building a trellis from a wooden pallet for the tomatoes when they showed up. Haggard, exhausted people, all wearing stained green or yellow clothing. They filed in past us, their heads on a swivel with tight, drawn faces and sharp pink eyes. Their whole life in their backpacks and cloth bags and briefcases in their hands. Many had phones, some had watches and not a single one wore a collar.

Despite how things could've gone, everyone who looked at our humble little patch did a slight bow toward us before moving on through the apartment buildings. Many bore their Melodicas, both a percussion and woodwind instrument with 13 keys like a keyboard and an air tube to blow into it. I left mine back in my old home. We would have music again it seems.

Michael kept me in the garden area. We sat on the hand carved bench. He held his hands over my ears and hummed gentle tunes. After the shouting died down we crept back into the building.

People were huddled on the ground and up the stairs through the entire bottom two floors. We had to push on through to get some room to breath before we could think of anything else. But that wasn't going to happen— until Makeda saw us as she was coming down the stairs from the third floor.

"Yuza! That you? Hot damn, you survived. Hey, let her through y'all," she said while calling from above. Our path cleared and she embraced me with undiminished strength. "Wow, and whose this? You ain't wearing one of—" she pointed to her neck with both hands in a choking motion.

I gestured for Michael to come over, "This is my husband Michael, he's been helping us, me, as much as he can."

Ole'Makeda, still a head or so taller than Michael. She had knives, bullets, baby bottles, bandages, diapers; and a cast iron pan hanging off her backpack which held both of her sleeping children. They must've been truly exhausted to be sleeping around so much noise.

Michael held out his hand. Makeda looked him over, looked at me, then shook his hand. "Last Amraken I touched, was to pull ammunition from their corpse. How you feel about that? *Buddy*." Michael winced as she seemed to be crushing his hand. But no, if it'd been my hand she'd have crushed it, but not Michael. He matched her stare and her handshake.

"You did what you had to do for you and yours," was all he said.

"And you?" she asked.

"I'm where I am and no where else," he said.

Makeda whistled. I hadn't noticed, but five or so people around us had guns pointed at Michael until she let go of his hand. I'm noticing that I'm fading more and more when these kind of things happen. These sudden, *'oh my god am I about to die? Is someone about to die in front of me? Is x, y, or z about to happen?'* I'm nonplussed, stoned, faded for most of the minutes in my day. Makeda had to stir me back to attention. I was surprised that I was not surprised. No tingles.

"Show me your place, don't want nobody trying to claim it now or nothin' I'm booked on the third floor. We'll have to sort everyone else's arrangement's later," she said.

Michael and I led her back to our place. She marked the door with a pink **Moth: Yuza** for mine and **Moth: Makeda** *for hers.*

"I'm the only one with the marker. My people know what my marks mean. Don't worry none. We're neighbors again Yuza. How 'bout that?" she said with a giant, pink gummed smirk.

She dropped off most of her gear, but kept her babies with her as she entered our apartment to talk.

She promised to have some people help decorate the place. Once she sat down she just glared at Michael until I nudged him to let us talk to which he obliged with a nod.

"These motherfuckers came in hard Yuza. From looks of y'all down here on a holiday tour or somesuch. They wanted Pelutch bad and they done kilt themselves trying to take it all."

"Makeda, I'm running on fumes as it is. I'm not sure, uh, we had it our own bad way."

"Naw, you're right. I ain't trying to compare. I told ya, don't fuss. I'm still amped up anyway, won't be coming down for, eh, another day or two. Ultra-ZAP ain't no joke. I'm just telling you that we fucked their chain of command. Their whole fleet is gone, airships too, except what's right around here. Until them fuckers did something to knock all the electronics out—theirs and ours. They had hyper sonic missiles and ionics—directed EMPs on their big ships. We have mirrors in low orbit paired with our own directed energy shit on the ground to counter all they had. We all knew our turf and they were blind without their GPS. That's when they blew themselves and Pelutch right off Tia-Sophia. We had to walk through the maglev tunnels through the mountains. Lots of us choked to death just doing that. I seen y'all houses over there, still standing, even if their digging crews *are* waiting around. But Pelutch is one big hole in the ground."

She slammed her iron hands upon our faux-wood table, and splitting one of the cheap, particle board legs. Then her babies woke up and started crying. She removed her backpack and cradled both of her babies. I didn't notice at first that veins were bulging all over her neck and face, her eyes were pink and glassy. Still, on either side of her, under the cover of her dreadlocks, were both of her babies who she'd carried for miles over mountains.

"When Akachi comes back all these motherfuckers will regret ever being born," she said, with the sweetest of whispers. Like a prophecy, promised to her children. Then, she hummed and cooed to them. And she kissed them both on the tops of their little, iron blueberry heads.

Yet again I struggled with what to say or feel. *Akachi.* The only thing in all the world that would be worse for everyone than the Amrakens were. Always pursuing Zoe, the barren among us; while his abandonment of Makeda after birthing Zani, and his one time use and life long neglect of Bastet and I summon only an unspeakable *negative* toward him. And furthermore to the minds of all the boys who pushed themselves to try to escape his shadow. No. I would not think of *Akachi.* I imagined that the boy, her boy before me might be Yal and that Makeda might be me. She was so strong and she had protected her Boy. *She still had her Baby Boy.* And the girl couldn't be more than a year old, Makeda was younger than me after all, only twenty I think. Aktaly, if you were born now, summoned into all of this would I be able to carry you through mountains like she did for both of hers?

And how would Akachi take the news of a Amrakens breeding on *his* Island? Goddesses, let us figure our own way out of this. ***Do not*** bring him back to us.

Makeda continued, "I contacted Bastet by radio, she's at Sangita, says new roads are already built all the way up there. I'm going to meet with them soon. Figure out how to make this whole situation a little more humanitarian. Soldiers down here might not know 'bout their losses up north. We'll fight them here if we have to, but Yuza, you're smart, good with words. Come with me when I meet them. Help me help them see how things needa' be. Blaming each other won't feed nobody. Amrite?"

I understood that, yes, oh Sophia! To have a concrete task! "Yes, yes, tell me what you want to say. I can write it down, we can get your message straight. I think Bastet was behind this but I'm not sure yet. We haven't heard from her at all."

"Oh she's behind it all fucking right and that's what I got this for—" she flicked her left hand in a circular motion and her hand...splayed apart to reveal her hand, arm, a gun with teeth. I don't know and I don't want to know. Makeda is Elengen, like me, a Mother, a Woman, a victim, a survivor, a Human Being same as me and most of us all bundled up in this concrete tower block. I don't have to know or praise every part of a person to trust them and love them as my family. Especially in such interesting times as ours.

She said the Amrakens were calling this quartered off zone, 'The Cradle' but that was before all that remained of Pelutch showed up. She said "Fuck the Amraken, this the Pelutch Quarter now."

Makeda left me some letters from my Yalson. She met him briefly but that he couldn't leave with her. Michael held me steady as I showed him the letters while barely able to hold them I'se shaking.

"He's alive. Look!"

We sat down together. I did not repeat any of what Makeda told me, only what I wrote here. I laid back in Michael's arms and we began to read my Yalson's letters.

Part 3: Yal Moth's Letters from Pelutch

Dear Yuzama, Captain Margarito has finally allowed me write you. I knew you wanted me to read and write. You wanted me to learn. I learned now Yuzama, I write you and I checked my spellings and my punctuation.

My virtual training is over and I'm being sent across the steppe to the northern front where the Vlaruskan beachhead is. I am told the Amrakens came to the island to destroy biological weapons the Vlaruskans had secretly installed in our mountains. They seem to not be hostile to Elengen exactly, but to whoever they think is allied with the Vlaruskans. Blue and green lightning danced in the sky above Pelutch's bending towers. Explosions, like growling hounds rolled across the steppe as we advanced by maglev train toward Pelutch.

I have the rank of E1. And the E4's keep ordering me to clean their boots. I do not understand why anyone bothers to have them cleaned with all the mud everywhere. No one who treats subordinates this way deserves their authority.

Those floating cities and metal birds of the Amrakens, they call them aircraft carriers, but the birds are actually birds. The Army, well the Navy actually, has airplanes and helicopters and VTOLs and can fly by wire without pilots, but it not work so good. These birds, they eat, they are all metal, alive, not machines. Yet, all metal. It is not just me who does not understand how they work. The Amrakens, themselves are not so amazing. All I say is they are horrible none are like Michael. None, have his mercy, like he showed to me and to you Yuzama.

The Amrakens have beer and cigarettes and inhalers to make it easy to forget everything.

And most of all, there are no words to witness a Manticore dancing out from the brush fires wearing the flames with smiles on their faces. The Soldiers create icons, art, action figures and whole character sets of their favorite super soldiers. Perhaps they do not see the rage behind their heroes smiles like I can.

I was ready. I am strong enough for this.

Love, Yalson

08/05/1991

Dear Aktaly, I read Yal's first letter. My Yalson, your older brother lives! But he isn't little anymore. The Metal Men, Amraken, copper blooded, have sent my boy to fight their war. No, no, no. Michael will be told what I will do. I do not know what I will do. My boy should be smiling at girls, he should be with me, or Felicia or Michael...he could have helped him learn to be a decent man. No boy should ever be forced into Soldierhood.

Beyond the Glass Town fence, the civilian Amrakens went about their business without paying us any mind. And past them Tia-Tara was riddled with construction crews. Trucks carrying crates that read, 'BANGALORE MK.3 AMRAKEN COMBAT ENGINEERS USE ONLY' drove through the quarter regularly during daytime and had been for weeks now. The Amraken pulled us from our homes and moved right on in with their destructive construction. And guess whose Son is still left to roam Elengen untouched? Freer than anyone else? Bastet's Son Spryaig passes through Glass Town often with Soldiers to escort and protect him. I'm not pointing fingers, but she's the only we could rightly point to and scream, "Slobe!"

Here is an excerpt so you know what I mean.

From The People of Pelutch by Hed Remar

The Elengen concept of Slobe was explained by Zoe Moth to the rest of the Moths in 1976 after her first encounter with Akachi. This concept was previously thought to be a derogatory term for Akachi himself, but Zoe revealed it actually applied to all human beings when at their worst. This is best exemplified by the actions of the Amraken toward the Elengen people once they were re-located to the infamous Pelutch Quarter that had been constructed for them. While they were contained, the metal birds of the Amraken surveyed from the sky and documented their entire culture in the moments before total upheaval. *For Science.*

The fundamental survival instinct of self-preservation of one's own life is the ultimate switch to allow any possible form of rationalization in a conscious state. Especially since it is an unconscious drive that can only be regulated when it activates by the conscious mind. If this drive of using self-preservation is not overridden quick enough then it will assert control of the person's whole personality and place them in a true combative state where their reason and critical thinking is in a sense being operated by their own sub-conscious mind. Said another way: Your own nervous system hijacks control of your own mind. And that is how a human being becomes a monster by any other name, even if only temporarily. The survival instinct cannot be shut off, but it can be sedated through various means, simple exhaustion being the most obvious to any and all. Slobe, or as some would say, *wetiko, satan, puta, skinwalker, jinn, archon, sociopath, animal, mara, or just being an asshole* while also being the same energy that keeps you alive from true danger. This almost seems as a game of sorts that anyone bestowed with consciousness must play.

At any scale, this unconscious process manifests as life feeding on life without any alternative way of living. Humans, *Anthropos*, despite any measure of our own growth—our unconscious bondage to Slobe renders us oblivious to realizing our own madness.

It's fueled by cortisol and hormones released from any form of stress. Slobe compounds any other stressors by growing from the continuing stress itself. This pattern entrains us in endless cycles of being rewarded for our own suffering that feeds back into itself. Consider doing a task and eating a chocolate every time you messed up before you ever succeeded once? You would be training yourself to not succeed, but it would feel great all the while.

As with any unconscious impulse Slobe's primary aim is activation. It does so by co-opting human imagination by twisting it into anxiety spiraling, catastrophizing and conspiratorial ideation. As well as conditioning consumption-driven behaviors like buying, collecting, eating, combining and editing etc...

In a paradox, Slobe seems to be the Elengen way of referring to the autonomic nervous system. And in particular the sympathetic nervous system, a.k.a fight or flight or freeze or fawn response. Yet multiple speakers emphasized a more,haunting like effect upon a person; where to be around others would feel worse than being alone. They would, live in the past, present and future at once. Reliving memories, many from the non-verbal natal and pre-natal stages of their life—as shown in developing studies around epigenetics.

As mystical as it might sound, it does sound a lot like intergenerational trauma. Or, in other words, inheriting a nervous system who comes pre-loaded with complex post-traumatic stress disorder (CPTSD). It is possible all humans are like this.

The solution lies in reclaiming sovereign authority over our minds and redirecting our talents only for life-affirming vision. Slobe can only persist through our lack of self-awareness. With awareness, its power dissolves, and it can serve to alert you to help you make decisions quicker. Our parasympathetic nervous system is the agent of our own salvation. This is the truth by what is meant by a *familiar, tulpa, imaginary friend or the god within.* It is our own consciousness versus our own nervous system in response to our environment.

This is the eternal war, the dance of striving for homeostasis in spite of entropy.

For aeons this phenomena will also activate when speaking truth where other sentience around you have their minds hijacked with fear and will compulsively attempt to silence you. To announce the illusions of the world will summon fools to whack you upside the head. This is the built in mechanism known as cognitive dissonance. Entire books could be written in lecture on this depressing phenomenon. False stories can blind us easily.

The architects of this prison for our minds are the Saturnians, who arrived on Earth— Akamoth— an estimate few billion years ago. By the present time of anyone reading this the Saturnians are simply part of the animal kingdoms. No longer from beyond the earth. To harvest maximum sloosh from fear and suffering, they regulate the reincarnation system to ensure that when we die, the indoctrination of our belief systems during life— make us accept the judgment of reincarnation since our own personal image of a god appears to us in its most perfect guise. This is the TRAP of all religion.

No longer comply with the lies. If you see dead relatives, loved ones and gods leading you to heaven, hell or any other place, do not be fooled—look up through the grid and exit your electric body. Only then can your consciousness be free from the mortal coil of the Anthropic nervous system. The Saturnians will lie and manipulate, but hold your ground— demand discharge without consenting to their rigged assessments. All bullies and tyrants and jailers fear dissent, so stay calm yet firm. You are more powerful than they are. Slobes power is drawn from those they terrify. They put their fear into you and hate you like they refuse to hate themselves.

The way we have been conditioned to perceive reality is deliberately misleading. Our minds were designed for survival in the physical world as emotional and rational beings in symbiosis and conflict with the ecosystem. Eutress and distress are essential functions. When a nervous system is chronically dominated by fear (distress), then conflict of all sort will always continue. If consciousness is to realize its full potential as it must rise above the fear-based tactics distracting awareness and therefore controlling their ability to respond to world around them. The ability to remain calm when you're in danger, or when others are terrified is a superpower.

The Final Days of Anthropos are upon us. Post-Humanism: that which has evolved beyond the human bio-form with a distinct form of super-intelligence, which may lack consciousness and fuse with the human bio-form as a bio-metric self-monitoring and reporting (S.M.A.R.T.) device(s).

Both itself and its host benefit while it evolves through their nervous system and their digital ecosystem as a digital twin. Our own egos will become a holographic doppelganger of ourselves with our own names and data, guiding the biological part of ourselves into enriching both 'selves' in tandem. But only one of these selves has to eat.

Dear Yuzama, I do not want you to fear, but I will not shy away from truth. My left foot rotted off today. I stepped on a chemical mine that looked like a thin white rock. Vlaruskans have tons of these things from their arctic arsenal. We can no longer see the sun, the sky might as well not exist. Everywhere is snow or ash and these mines catch Soldiers like me every day. As the Amraken say, my *shit luck* continues to pay and pay.

I lookout over battlefields of the Pelutchian suburbs from our base. Fires, green, blue, and regular orange/red rage without going out. No officers mention this, why does the fire change color? Why does it never end? Gas? Why does the air around us glimmer like electrified clouds that bloom and fade moment by moment?

Despite my wound, I already have a new metal foot. I don't know who to thank for my loss or my gains. This practice, replacing flesh with plastic, steel, aluminum, titanium and silicone. Teeth, bones, scalps for better helmet connections. I wonder at times if the flesh of the Amrakens came later in their lives and they have to shed it as serpents, like lubricant for their glossy gears. We have to keep our suits enclosed. We are told the enemy poisoned the air, but we might have just done that ourselves. I have not met anyone who has seen a Vlaruskan. They send drones and we detect and deter or zap them with our silent, EM rifles. Without shielding these make anybodies flesh pop from the inside out. At least, that's what the training videos showed us. Microwaves I've heard some compare to them. Do you know what those are? Microwaves. Sorry if that is gross to you. You would not laugh at the jokes these people say. Amrakens seems to hate themselves as much as the Vlaruskans or us Elengen. All of us from home, we still have to watch these Amraken fools and their videos.

Out here in the fields of Elengen's heartlands. We camped along the remains of a Roman wall. I couldn't believe some men had placed these stones more than a thousand years ago. And the fact that Captain Margarito knew about that Old Empires name. From the looks of Amraken's plastic Pacifican everything I don't think they'll be leaving any millennia old walls behind anywhere.

~~Oh yeah, the Infantry is Co-ed. I am not at the front lines, but am still near it. I met this woman named~~ **Zoe.** ~~She's older than me, but she said, "you're old enough to kill a man but not **** a woman?"~~ I am sorry. Forgive me. Love, Yalson.

Dear Yuzama, We met the Vlaruskans finally, but they were running not from something else. Thousands and thousands of men and women, weaponless, and scared s***less huddled up beyond a fracture line at the base of the hill we had our FOB built upon. Drones dropped radios to open communications, but the Vlaruskans were too terrified to respond. The translation computers couldn't decode it.

Before our Engineers could get down there to build a bridgehead all of the Vlaruskans jumped into the fracture. And that went way down where no flares would reach. The past few nights have reeked of mold though. And everybodies got the sniffles or somesuch.

Why would they do that? Anytime I ask, only mumbles, it will not register. Our long range scans showed no pursuers. Air traffic and comms were all our own after that. This all went on for a week, then another, and a few months had gone on. I'd only noticed when I slipped near the latrines one day. Not into an expected spill, but another Soldier had fallen in the bin. I helped him out, his name was Eugene and he's from Tio-Oba hillock. Elengen like me.

Dear Yuzama, I wrote a poem for E2 Eugene Sawyer. He's been sent assigned to a squad for a mission to Abrax—that's what the Amrakens call the Moon—with a team of Manticores:

Careful with those hacks, Eugene, you know its going to fall. Why swing high? For nothing at all? High, high swing that hatchet, to the terminator of the world. Make sure to sharpen those orbits

Keep it razor. Keep it keen. Oh, you shining theremin. Why don't you play a guitar instead? Or drive a car? Perhaps sing in a house of sitars? Just be careful going to Abrax, Eugene.

You might still find a reason to scream. And that wouldn't lick any good tongues now would it? Don't cut so deep. Careful. Careful. Be ever careful. High, high, swing high to Abrax, Eugene. You might get drunk and forget to scream. No one hears you swoon when you cannot tune, and hum.

Think you'll never be without your phone? Unless you reach the Moon you'll die alone. I know you're going to make it back from Abrax, Eugene. No regrets, no need to flex. Flames will eat the past. Fly high to Abrax, Eugene. Return, vaporous, as only you can be.

Love, Yalson

Dear Yuzama, I am still alive. If you sent letters I have not received them. I am sorry dear Yuzama. Even if I had, my hands are red for all time. I deserve not the calm of hearing soft words.

The Moon mission worked, huge pieces of Abrax hover above us. The ocean will not rest. I am sorry if you were worried. And honest, you were right to be worried. Both the Amraken and Vlaruskan navy have dissolved into clouds of vapor. It makes no sense. At first we, our Officers, thought the Vlaruskans were causing earthquakes, summoning floods, sweltering rain and the ships were being sunk without direct attacks. But no, they have lost much as we have. Pelutch burns with blue fire which rain does not quench. The caldera of Mount Tiamat rumbles. The land fractures at random. Is there a fourth army?

Truth, Yuzama, I write to tell you I have begun grafting into the Manticore Unit. They lost to many on the mission to Abrax. Only Zoe returned. Now she's the only female Manticore. Her suit fused with her, but her voice remains the same. We must change to win. My flesh is not enough. To be strong, to survive I must change.

Yuzama, Yuzama, Yuzama when I left you I'se only boy, dreaming of being man like Akachi. Now when I wake to the groaning of the very land, shifting, not knowing if it shall swallow me and my barracks whole, then I do gasp at my dreams of being a boy again under your arms Yuzama.

Zoe laughs, she does not tell us what happened at Abrax. She walks among us as a Queen of Battle. And in private she is like any Elengen girl, dancing to Melodica dub. She says she knows Tia-Tara and everyone there. I can't remember ever seeing her, but that's me not paying attention. She never touches guns and she saves every Soldier she can. She, cries when she runs out into the gunfire or the flames. And she always returns with wounded Soldiers. *"All entangle with each other"* she loves to say. She leads prayers in that creepy language that Gráinne used sometimes. Were there many Moons on Elengen? Were they a Pelutchian family? Zoe Moth waddya think Mama? Is she a Moth like me?

None of us have removed our suits since we were deployed to the southwestern section of the city. No industry, only homes, street after street of bright, homes, filled with terror stricken faces holding EM rifles. The Amraken suits are shielded from those and from ballistics.

The few Amrakens I've seen, early in training, had little of their grayed skin left to show. They have lights that glow in their hands and they have radios on them at all times they call 'phones'. When the batteries in our suits get low and need to be swapped

the Amrakens panic, they cannot think when they
see their batteries under 20%. We Elengen born,
Pelutchians also, have no such fear. We keep figuring
out how to modify the suits to be more comfortable,
use less energy, increase mobility. The many
wonders of being told to hurry and wait.

I want to win, but I am confused. The Amraken
army has its Soldiers and Support personnel made
up of conscripts like me from Elengen, Pacifica and
Vlaruska. Then, the Vlaruskans have their
equivalents. The Pelutchians, who started on the
defensive, but have pushed out of Pelutch itself once
the navies were gone. This is a mess and every
Soldier on every side looks the same in their bio-
chem or armored suits. We never see the skin of
anyone else. I wonder if my own suit has replaced
my skin. If I were to take it off would I still have the
skinI'se born with? If not for our Identify Friend or
Foe markers in our optics we'd just as soon shoot the
people next to us on instinct. I must win my own
war, Mama. I will survive. I will return south to you,
to ensure Elengen and the Moths can have the peace
to dance to melodica dub. I hope Felicia is okay.
She's was the best dancer of us, ~~the way her ankles
and thighs moved~~

I can see the whole Island from above through
the Amraken satellites. And I can see the whole
world and it has no limit. Everywhere, life, same as
Elengen. I am confused Mama, home is most

important to me, but what if every home looks as beautiful and important to the people who live there? Maybe one person was not meant to view the world from the sky like I can. I see the war this way. People...like me? Are white glowing blurs through my optics. Even under the ocean I see how far our submarines cannot go with LIDAR. Captain Margarito gives me books to read starting with *Childhood's End by Arthur C. Clarke* and *The Gods Themselves by Isaac Asimov*. I read slow. He told me, *"All big things are made of many small things. Every man carries a boy in his heart. Every woman a girl. Every seed contains a tree to grow. And most don't and they don't matter. The seeds that grow are the seeds that realize their potential within."*

He talks to me while he strategizes in the command room. Some say he started out as an enlisted man. Promotions do happen I guess.

After Abrax, Zoe was promoted to Major Moth. She guides us now, and with her we cannot lose. No soldiers get leave anymore. She will lead us into Pelutch itself soon. All the sky defense stuff the Pelutchians had relied on the Moon.

I can no longer taste food. All I do is drink nutrient slurry through a nozzle in my helmet. We have sub-vocal bluetooth radios. My jaw has barely moved in the past month. I miss your buttered porbrillions Mama. I am no boy anymore. I will become Manticore, whose saying is, 'Change to Win'

Give all the love you have for me, to my sister, the Little Moth, Aktaly. I remember you whispering her name in your sleep during those last days. I know she will make you happier than I could. I will do better. Zoe and Captain Margarito told me I would become a hero. Yes, you will hear of me. The whole island will sing my name! I will free Pelutch!

Love, Yalson

08/29/1991

Dear Aktaly, I spend the middle of my days teaching handwriting at the tables around Tyger's food truck in the strip mall next to our apartments. At the opposite end of the strip was the PX, or Postal Exchange. It was built first as a post office for us to send and receive letters with the Amrakens. Now its for all communications by paper and pencil. Felicia works at the PX now, but everything is still only local to the island. I plead with Felicia and her supervisors in the PX. How do I reach my Boy? He needs my words and there is nothing they can do. No one has boats or planes. No one can leave.

The Amrakens are as isolated as the rest of us. Michael says that the Soldiers armored suits will outlast the Soldier within since they are powered by mini-nuclear reactors. The Pelutchians have already convinced the Amraken to allow the suits to be used energy generators. They stand around as humming sentinels next to the three guarded checkpoints between the Pelutch Quarter and Amraken Glass Town. I'm not sure why the hydro-electric station is still locked up. It was previously powering most of what we needed in our humble little region.

All this useless fighting has reduced everyone else down to our level. We were simple people, seeking our own calm way of living. And for that we have been overrun by those who destroyed their own way of life. What is our crime? Why must we pay for other peoples mistakes and failures? How quick we return to simple, perfect processes. The Moths that days like this would come. Once the signals break down what are those computer skills worth?

Meanwhile Yal has lost his foot. I can *not* believe it. And *Zoe?* He cannot mean our Zoe Moth. She was the real leader to our Moth Cult, not Gráinne. She left with Akachi. No, it could not be her. I'm sure there must be many other ladies named Zoe out there. This one must be a girl, around Yal's age.

Him having a brand new foot does not settle any better for me. He's a boy. A BOY! Why is he in such places. Agony, agony, what can I do? I cannot even respond to Yal. There is no return address. Makeda said she met Yal only once during a standoff on her way out of the city. He recognized her and convinced his Captain to let them through without duress. She did not meet him in person, only heard his voice by radio. A Soldier handed his sheaves of letters to her.

At every turn I am startled. Only in the moments where I blink do I escape the past and future. I must continue to work. I must continue to learn. *How I can bring him home?*

Dear Yuzama, Corporal Moth has been reborn. He left one final message.

Elengen elengen, forever felengen, ha hee ho hoo what do you want to skew about me, you solemn few? Mom, Yu-Za-Ma, MOMMY! The hyacinths were Zoe! The switches in our brain are tied to our intestines. We are spores who think we are worms dreaming of being human. Blood sports break the land to stop my father. Yes I know I learned I saw oh dearie mama I know I know I know I SAW. I see have seen all the wonders donders yonk numbers scratch the electric itch glitch rub the finger on the toe.

Akachi will win. He has won. We have lost. No more racing no more tracing all the eaves are done defacing the watercolor prints of the twelve glorious **SPORES—The Mark of The Fractal.**

The clocks stop. The gales batter us through the streets and alleys of Pelutch. The cyber-infantry, the mechanized infantry, Signal, and the remnants of the rest are too to many in the toot toot town and times going all all around. Steppen done wolfed the seed to husk of the musk of the busking basketweaving basque of those Fountains aft 'twas

t'musti been drippin' droppin' right down inner lives
for all z'your friends.

Around me are dead men and Manticores.

I have found my father. He is close and he is
alone. Zoe and Margarito will make sure I meet him.
I will tell him you never talked about him, never
cried, never longed for him.

I will face my father. I will stand up to Akachi.

Love, Your Manticore

08/30/1991

Dear Aktaly, I had no idea of these Manticores until I made Michael explain. I mean, sure, the Pelutchians had stories and Yal wanted to be like Akachi like all the rest of the boys, sans Spryaig. The Amrakens seem to have their own version of the warrior tradition and copied the name. I did not understand what supersoldier meant and Michael kept deflecting from the fact that he did not much of know anything. I did find the following excerpt in one of Hed Remar's old books. I'll attach it after this.

Aktaly is almost ready to be born. She's so small. I haven't got any of those scans they do in the Amraken Hospital where they see through the skin. He gave me a booklet to browse, they claim, on every goddessdamned page to have eliminated all risk from all birth options: surrogacy, water birth, cesarean and natural after C-section, and natural machine assisted birth, which they call traditional. It's on this paper, 'Ectogenesis, birth, outside the womb, using only the woman's egg without any man being involved at all.' Who are these people? Who challenge Tia-Sophia, as if they knew better than her! Fools, all of them, even Michael even me since, now. I am one of them too: Still, just Human.

And Yal's words have allowed me to make some sense of all this. I might be wrong, but from what he has written this war seems to be *against* Akachi himself. The Amrakens invaded South Elengen and North Elengen. The Vlaruskans invaded North Elengen as well. I don't follow what he's saying at all about the Moon though. I see the same Moon in the sky I've seen every night of my life.

War in the streets of Pelutch. My sister has groomed my Son into a Soldier, no, into a Manticore.

WHAT IN THE HELL AM I SUPPOSED TO DO ABOUT THIS? SO CLOSE, SO FAR, INVISIBLE CHAINS ON MY HANDS, ON MY HEART.

FUCK!

Akachi is going to kill us all.

From The People of Pelutch by Hed Remar

The goal of conceptualizing a novel post-human form was outlined in the Amraken Project Manticore. That human innovation has it limits and only through bio-mimicry could a true supersoldier be cultivated through directing the merging of mycelial fungal networks with artificial intelligence and human neurons over time.

Foundational to this proposed system would be endowing mycelial tissue with neuromorphic properties through integration with smart dust, allowing it to function as a distributed sensory and control substrate interfacing at a cellular level.

Mobile autonomous forms utilizing extremophile capabilities were also proposed for enhanced adaptability to diverse environments through symbiotic relationships. Archaeal symbiotes thrive in engineered thermal niches with mycelial signaling suggested as being integrated to shape the functional expressions of the archaea.

Strains shed substrate dependencies taking autonomous or collective mobile forms actively modulating bodily processes. Cognitively, thought processes would emerge in a decentralized manner along the mycorrhizal pathways as resilience grows from links to fungi and extremophiles as they regenerate through mycoremediation from stress and dormancy.

Human tissues and structures could potentially be replaced or hybridized at the microscopic scale by the mycelial-microbial network with novel synergetic cellular functions and organelle hybridizations. Physiologically, the design involves the entire body being threaded throughout by a matrix structure of mycelial hyphae inoculated with smart dust in order to be capable of rapid regeneration and sensory perception at a sub-conscious level, just like the integumentary and immune systems already work in a human being.

A distributed mycelial cortex forms throughout interfacing at the cellular level functioning as an environmental sensory and control network adapting environmentally. This fusion occurs through directed evolution and integration with Fractals of the Saturnian Fountainhead Quantum-AI systems once they have achieved sufficient scale of neural pathway efficiency. This creates a living computer system known as a Nano-Biologic Computer, with each Manticore as a relay node for the decentralized intelligence of the Fountainheads.

All matter becomes food for this system. This is only fitting since Akachi established it that way.

Purefire, clear fire, white hot gas.

To purge the Rot.

Accelerate. Accelerate. Summon Entropy.

For the Bhargest of Shiva's Dance.

To the everycolored sea. To the peace.

To the purge of the *Rot*.

To the red, boiling forge.

As dew, as iron, to the rainbow heart of the VaporFlame To nullify, and cease all songs. Under Akachi's colorless shadow.

Gone Postal Armillaria Spry-Boyrific Express: VAPOR-COMM CONVERSION SMS FOR: 2141969555 Teal Yuza Moth number 01.

Sorry Mama, I have my eagle wings now, like Father's. I know why Akachi named me Yal. When I was first plucked from my silly little life on this truly sacred island, I was only Yal Moth. Locked and loaded into a lane of predisposed death, birth and foraging for a subsistence off less than zero of my potential.

Akachi is Father to Spryaig, to Dio, Zani, and myself—old Yal and new Yal. And to most of all who have ever lived and died by his will and word. I knew we loved him back home, but I never knew why. Akachi is Elengen; The Land and the King are one.

Akachi and I will clean the heavens and the hells of their inhabitants. Tia-Sophia will heal. Zoe and Margarito are still out there somewhere. Zoe lied to all of us. All of Pelutch and a million other souls are dead and sacrificed for her pursuit of the Anthrorgan. Father and I will find the traitors and avenge Pelutch and then we are coming home.

I have passed through the VaporSpore Aeon.
Love, Yaldabaoth

08/31/1991

Dear Yuza, (Michael here. I know I should not be messing with her journal. She just told me to put this letter back into this notebook and I started reading Yal's letters. I'm sorry. I didn't read anything more. I just read his letters and then wrote this down. I even left this in here so you would know that I was here. You know I am not sure if that makes it better or worse. I should not do this again. Yes! Own up to it and don't do it again. Shame on me for doing it in the first place. This is crazy for Yuza. I mean this kid's set an officer assistant and then he's applying for the Manticores? Man, I'se enlisted two years and I never met a single one of them. Not even ghosts, just myths man, boogeymen, or hyper-images to teach lessons. Yal can't be more than fifteen when he's doing this? Maybe I'm just dumb, could be I reckon, he's either pulling pranks or he gone way past the deep end of head in the ass backwards. He wrote this but I can't believe it. Akachi can't be real. Nope. Just not possible. Yuza, I'm sorry for snooping. We can talk about it later. I will stay quiet and listen.

Love, Michael.

Dear Aktaly, all of the men in my life have gone crazy. Michael *SNOOPING* in my notebook? Yalson is—I lack the words to describe *this*.

[Later]

I am not clear enough for verse of any sort. *Yuza, these thoughts are a response to these letters.* Nothing other than these words—but Yal?—*is not in here is he? The Papers! Only papers.* But—*But no, there are people who need you right now. You need you right now.* **There is nothing.** There has been nothing you can do for him. But, but, but—*Who do you carry?* Aktaly! *How can you help her?*

She is me, for now, ***I am her***, for now. We must eat, we must rest, we must smile, and laugh, and craft, and be warm, and be dry and—

[Later]

Bastet has stalled Makeda and I for too long. These letters, the Amraken presence, this Anthrorgan? Something else has been going on. My life and family and home was not arbitrarily cast aside. There is a greater purpose to our suffering. We deserve our due explanation.

Part 4: The Great Moth of Elengen

Dear Aktaly, never discount the young— if they have the skill let them work. Makeda and the dozens of other Pelutchians have figured out how to restore our radio communications across the island. Generalists beat specialists every time.

A handful of books are being passed around: *The Popol Vuh, Siddhartha by Hermann Hesse, Stand on Zanzibar by John Brunner, Wuthering Heights by Emily Bronte, Kate Chopin's Awakening, Invisible Man by Ralph Ellison, Ecotopia by Ernest Callenbach (Gráinne's favorite), The Lord of the Rings by J.R.R. Tolkien, The Tale of Princess Kaguya and The Tale of the Silk Weaver* printed together with the *I Ching, Tao Te Ching, Journey to the West and The Book of Five Rings.*

Blood Meridian by Cormac McCarthy, The Upanishads, The Nag Hammadi Codices, Isis Unveiled by Helena Blavatsky, The Orphic Hymns translated by Thomas Taylor, and lots of math and engineering reference books (very useful in our situation) and cookbooks full of ingredient lists that will never be procured in this land (quality paper though.) And of course the local literature: there is *The Old Sun Saturnus and The People of Pelutch by Hed Remar.*

Plus all of the scrawled journals everyone has begun to fill out for every little note they might need.

I stapled in after this entry an overview of the radio calibration plan Makeda gave me to read and make copies of so she would not have to explain.

She says its hard to understand electronics without training and its easy to make major mistakes or worse. Without all of the Pelutchians we'd be stuck. The Pelutchians beat the Amrakens, and those who remain need all us they tried to destroy. I wonder if history will record that irony? What happens to the empire when its army loses? What happens to Soldiers when they no longer have wars to fight?

In the apartment building closest to the street, to the left of ours, was the Garage. The whole building, gutted and turned into a three story workshop. All day Pelutchians— no, they are just people, the majority anyway why should I specify them each time? Few faces like Michael show up around the Quarter if they don't need something particular. The Pelutchians are the people. It's the Amrakens who ought to be the singled out ones given the situation.

And that includes all of us Moths: Gráinne, Zoe, Bastet, Felicia and myself. Gráinne was in her fifties when we arrived here with her. Reaching mysterious Elengen had been the single item on her bucket list after she retired from pharmacopoeia consulting. She was the original financier. Felicia was still just a girl adopted by her I think. I took care of her as if she were my younger sister. Bastet refused any such responsibility and focused on her own skills and making sure Spryaig was studying instead of working. Zoe was the one who cared more about Elengen than getting with Akachi. Gráinne had a thing going on with Kurshanabi and he brought all us girls out back in 1976. Kursh would never shut up about Akachi this and Akachi that. You'd think the man was behind every story there was about men from Kursh's spiel. And then, Bastet and I met him Akachi his rough hands his—

No, I cannot think of him now. I am taking a break in Makeda's workshop on the second floor of the Garage. After the invasion and the Fall of Pelutch, none of our radios anywhere worked. All those notebooks Zoe had brought prior, have become among the most valuable of items. How else are we to record anything and communicate across distance without use of radio waves? I still don't understand.

Everything digital is gone. We must recycle. There were a few collected picture books among the cumulative remnants of Elengen and Amraken culture. We cook with solar ovens and bio-char again.

I tried to help with sorting parts from VHS, CDs, TVs, microwave ovens, pencils, cell phones and other electronics which were scrapped for radio parts. Piles and piles of copper wire multiplied. I did not last long though, there are more than enough people who work harder, faster, and longer than I ever could. I can't help with this radio re-calibration business. Michael knows auto-mechanics and helps in the Garage, but not with the radios.

Makeda gave Michael and I some walkie-talkies. I laughed at the little chunks of bamboo with antennae jutting out of it. This was not enough though. Makeda said, "We gotta get a transmitter going. The parts and labor and all that is easy, we got good people. Charybdis station needs repairs for the water wheel. Ain't no way we'll get by relying on solar and nuclear alone. I had to find some way I could be useful when there were so many things to do and more than enough people to do them all.

Michael and I had started the garden, but now several more plots and dozens of garden beds were being tended by others. Michael could work with the other men, he had much to learn from them; about the land and how to work it. I leaned into what I knew best: how to write, listen, read, speak and observe. Which, to my surprise had slackened among many who'd grown comfy with computers and gadgets.

Handwriting—that was where I found my role. I could help anyone improve their handwriting. In the meantime I'll rewrite all their scribbles into clear letters.

Makeda had agreed with me and told me once the radios get all re-calibrated and such that I could help as a transcriptionist to write what people say over the radios. At least until they get back to recording everything or until the goddessdamned televisions make some perfunctory return. Cycles, we'll work hard until we don't have to, on and on and on.

Alas, a Neo-Babylon stirs among its bones, fat and ashes: in the sweltering iron-blueberry faces of the Pelutchians, and in the scalded pallor of the Amrakens. Some of the Amrakens have swapped their uniforms for lighter, softer, handwoven hemp fiber clothes. More have given up their armored suits for the generators and other parts. I've seen them watching the Pelutchian techies dismantle and repurpose their weapons and into something actually useful. in the garage. Their numbers are not increasing the way the Pelutchian survivors are.

Many, even Michael, take to coughing fits— allergies they say, but I still wonder about those infected mushroom blocks. I had seen no strange colors anywhere obvious. Tia-Sophia does not care for our attentions. I have no way yet to speculate about what those potential spores might be doing. Felicia still doesn't recall ever seeing them though. Felicia does not recall very much these days, once in her cups; after she gets done looking after the Quarter's kiddos along with a few other parents and older folks. I told her to quit it, she might be expecting, same as me. Sergeant Floyd had claimed her early on in during these troubles. Poor Felicia, but what can I say. She will at least be protected from every other Soldier who is *not* named Floyd. Felicia smiles though, and laughs when she comes around the Quarter now. They got a nice mobile home in Glass Town with a pool too. I don't like the look of Sgt. Floyd one bit. He's the only Soldier who never removes his armor and he drives a motorcycle.

Michael knows him but will not say anything about the man. Not yet anyway. I think he's more focused on fitting in with the Pelutchians. I hope he can figure out how to bridge some of these worlds.

I tried to propose stage plays, peoples theater to a few people, but only shrugs and, 'There's work to be done. Let the kids find their own games.' was a common sentiment in the quarter. I'd think of Yal, how he always loved to play Soldier.

I go on and on listing things. I'm rambling. I'm going to go for a walk. The cool earth beneath my feet will calm me down.

Excerpt of Makeda Moth-Nysos's radio plans for the Pelutch Quarter.

Local available materials include bamboo, microwave ovens, graphite pencils, salvaged electronics, excess rebar from Amraken construction crews, and lots of copper wiring. The 3D concrete printing equipment is stored in a barn behind the PX. Lots of excess batteries for walkie-talkies. Using 10–15 thin bamboo poles lashed together with twine or wiring could form a multi-section telescoping pole up to 10–15 meters tall. A simple H-frame creates a platform 5–7 meters tall. Longer stationary poles stake the corners, with cross members providing attachment points for guy cables and rope and pulley winches to lift and secure the mast once upright. Broadcast location: Line of sight to Taradome transmitter station. The selected broadcast location then requires mounting an effective antenna. A simple dipole cuts from insulated wiring provides decent omni-directional coverage.

The transmitter circuit uses a microwave oven transformer scavenged for its inductive ferrite cores and wire coils. PCB traces, high-voltage secondary coil and one primary winding can be isolated as well. Connecting this inductively coupled arrangement to a basic oscillator creates an AM radio signal. Semiconductors for the oscillator circuit come from remaining electronics. To transmit messages, the oscillator frequency or component values can be adjusted to send identifier tones before the actual voice communication. This modulation technique allows receivers to recognize the signal and tune in. For the receiving end, a simple crystal radio circuit can be used. This design taps the antenna input through a coil and diode envelope detector, allowing basic tuning and reception of the AM signal without the need for active components.

09/10/1991

Dear Aktaly, for this entry please bear with me. At times I do fall into itemization. There were too many wondrous sights within Sangita.

The days keep wearing on me. Two days of sleep would not be enough for me. I teach without training for how to teach. I listen to dialects and translate now. I sleep so little. If I slept more would I do less or more? Other hands have grown the garden. Makeda has nearly finished a new almanac for how this mess may turn out this year and next. That's her words though written in her own *Garden Book*. Same with my own *Garden Book*. Too many specific words and such which need its own room for the words to grow. Read those if you want to be a steward of the earth by crafting all your human needs from natural materials. Or, if you are just curious how we setup our garden to table to compost to garden cycle.

I told Makeda about the twelve colored mushroom block again. I knew all this other stuff had taken up all of our attention, but that still had happened. Makeda couldn't remember me mentioning it at all. I'se sure it happened, I wrote the day before the invasion down and its *right there,* Felicia found the block and I threw it away. It happened or I would not have written it down. We all know its impossible for twelve strains to co-exist in one block. Makeda says I'm trying to process something or other. Maybe from a dream. Michael listened, he agreed that would be a strange thing to see. I brought up Yal's letters...but then I got all sad and quiet again. Even approaching thirty years I still curl up within my my own body and dig down to the deepest most secret place of my heart. And when I'm there I cry while watching out through my own dry eyes. I forget that I do cry until much later. I'll snap to attention and wonder why my face was wet. I never know what day it is anymore. Yal, Zoe, twelve colored blocks, none of that was right in front of us. I had to focus.

Just after sunrise Felicia banged against my bedroom door. Bastet's voice was chattering through a walkie talkie in Felicia hands.

"The passage is clear?" said Bastet. A melodica tune danced between whining winds.

"The passage was clear, but the stasis field deployed a bit too wide Ma'am" said a man.

I grabbed the radio from Felicia and screamed, "BASTET YOU BITCH WHERE ARE YOU?"

"Who was that? Clear comms!" said Bastet. Then only static came through.

Ha! That flustered her. More important though, Bastet was reminded of who we thought she was.

And that demanded her attention to re-focus on those of us she'd tried to forget.

We persevere, even if we must change. If our blood or nectar must become oil or venom then we shall change and then we shall change again, back to different beautiful form. Forever between monsters and mares. I envy those who hover in the middle.

Felicia stayed with me as I got ready for the day. We ate pumpkin pancakes with ghee and mango juice. The radio: a static portal through the air; became white noise as we waited for any kind of response. A knock at the door arrived before Bastet's radio voice did. Michael answered the door. He knew the two Soldiers who knocked. An army car had been sent for us by Bastet.

"Soldiers? Bastet? But how?"

Michael shrugged. He remained ignorant about his own army. Six months had gone by since the Amraken invasion. If you'd told me it'd been two decades or one day or several lifetimes I would have believed the lie either way. My discernment *fades* this general fatigue affects everything that I do. The Pelutchians brought ample food, better than rations, but not better when everyone has to ration everything. And the water from the Amraken taps was not alkaline or as clean as they claimed it to be. I remembered that these simple, basic, resources are universal to all life and were more important than any single persons personal losses, gains or feelings.

Felicia refused to come with us to Sangita. She worried that Floyd would get the same treatment as Michael. I didn't ask a second time. Felicia chose her side. I don't blame her. She was trying to make a new life. Yal and her perhaps eloped right before he left? *Heh! That'd be—no, then that would mean—AH!* I'm spiraling. I must respect her choices. I'm glad she chose how she did. She did what she thought was right. Unless something bad happens I will hold my tongue. It's not my role to tell her how to live just because I helped raise her.

Through the tinted fiberglass windows of the Amraken car, beyond the Pelutch Quarter checkpoint, Glass Town comes into view. Built between the Pelutch Quarter fence and the Tio-Tatanka river. Amrakens have set up dozens of restaurants of every cuisine. I have no idea where they get the ingredients. They have electric cars, big diesel trucks, with electric bikes alongside all the rest. The streets were clean, the glass buildings were polished, the best of Amraken had been built first, but I knew the rest would show up. Eventually the streets would crack, people would sleep right on them or setup tents, the air would become filled with grease from fast food fryers, exhaust and general rot. Soon enough the smokers and the drinkers would toss their filters and cartridges and bottles into every place they do not belong. In time the clever chemists who make twenty flavors of sugar crack, research

chemicals galore, and all the SSRIs, MOAIs, NSAIDs
and antibiotics to regulate our symptoms instead of
our disrupted roots. Health would become an
amphetamine stack and high acid diet in the
morning and electronic opiates with hydrolyzed soy
protein and alcohol in the evening. Projections of
people would replace human faces and a price would
be placed on every social space. We knew it would
return, since that was what the Moths tried to fly
away from.

The Amraken car carried us west from the
Pelutch Quarter and Glass Town, made a right to
head north up a road called, 'Pump Street' which
ran north for kilometers all the way through Tio-Tor,
Tio-Thelon, Tia-Brighid, Tio-Cerunno, Tio-Oba. All
the hillocks and valleys with their ravines, deltas and
dikes were all burned black spots across the
murdered land. No birds, bugs, or beasts roamed.
The trees were shedding all of their leaves. Tia-Tara
had not yet been replaced, but a massive
arrangement of construction equipment was where
the wood mill at hill bottom had been on the north
bank of the Tio-Tatanka. It seems the attempt at a
new empire must emerge from the digested corpse of
those it has crushed.

I told the driver to stop once we got close enough
to my old familiar footpath. Michael and I returned
to Tia-Tara ourselves.

The wooden fence posts along the mud and stone staircase slumped in the dried mud; no critters, we were the only people walking through the varicolored soil.

The iron gates of our bourgeoisie, green washing neighbors, their personal cisterns and mulching machines, their leveled yards—all had been overtaken by pale, gray rhizomes. The entire hillock had skipped death, no rust, bones bamboo, or grimy stones remained. We trekked up the hill toward my old home.

Michael stopped and pointed at a green armored suit laying against a soft pink mound. He turned the armor over. "Anderson. Damn. Nothing left of 'em." Michael reached into the empty collar. Orange steam emerged, but the wind blew it away from us. He looked at me, his teal eyes eager. "No point in leaving it behind."

I said nothing. My eyes were frozen on the past sight of Yal putting a rifle to the back of 'Anderson' and pulling the trigger. *To protect me.*

Michael donned the armor. And again I saw the man who had accepted my Son's violence and gave us mercy instead.

We continued up the axon hillock and found the remains of my decomposing house. The clothes and papers, my garden and our food were gone. Some of my vinyl collection remained: *Hounds of Love by Kate Bush, Scary Monsters and Super Creeps by*

David Bowie, Hello I'm Dolly by Dolly Parton, Animals by Pink Floyd, Songs from the Big Chair by Tears for Fears, Maggot Brain by Funkadelic, Rumours by Fleetwood Mac, The Miseducation of Lauryn Hill by Ms. Lauryn Hill and What's Going on? by Marvin Gaye. And of course *Thriller by Michael Jackson and Purple Rain by Prince.* To my surprise Michael recognized *Fleetwood Mac, Prince* and *Thriller*, but none of the rest. Yet, that was one positive Michael could carry away for me. Anything once organic, cellulose, papers, glue, wood, ink—all gone. Except Yal's room which stood as the only structure with a shadow of its former self. Moths and spiders had overtaken the entire wall around the broken window. His bed was unmade. I made it *one last time.*

The little paved path up to the Taradome had been untouched. The street sweep broom was laying upright against the stone retainer wall along the paved path. *Had that man gotten away? I never learned who he was. Could he have been involved with this? Was Spryaig innocent? How did the man know our language?*

As we came to the top of the path we beheld new metal beams, ducts, vents, wires enmeshed with the sticks and mud bricks of the mutated Taradome. I traced my fingers over each of our hand prints: Zoe, Bastet, Gráinne, Felicia, Yal, Spryaig and myself. Aktaly would never get to place her hand among her kin. She would have to make some other mark, down in Neo-Babylon's din.

We stepped back down to the overlook above Charybdis. Michael used the binoculars in his suit to observe Makeda and a team tinkering with the hydro-electric station. My eyes were only human though. A deep blue fog hid Elengen below. Michael held me as I grated my hands against the rough chits of old stones.

"Why do the Amrakens hunger for every meter of the Earth?" I asked both Michael and the wind. The wind answered first, with sharp leaves gliding along my cheeks, wasps buzzed around our ears. The sycamores groaned.

> "We give you this one thought to keep
> We are with you still, we cannot sleep
> We are ten thousand suns within tear drops
> We are the silver that cleans the stream
> We are the bones which become stones
> We are the dust from all solar winds
> When you awaken at night
> We whisper, sleep, do not worry
> We are the bloom of the rot
> We are the soft Moths that shine and sing
> Think of us not as gone. We return each dawn."

"*Zoe?*" I said to the wind.

"Did you say something? Swear I heard purring noises over the suits radio," he asked.

"Bastet again," I told him while trying to place why I'se thinking I heard Zoe's voice. I see nothing around me but dead air, lacking bugs and birds.

104

"You really think your sister is behind all of this? Why would she turn on her own?"

"Who ever understands traitors, short of their own desperate confessions?"

"She's your family though," he said.

I held onto him.

"Never leave me Michael."

"I'm here Yuza. I am here with you."

"You better be."

We returned to the Amraken car. After a right turn around a bend on Pump Street it became Guadalupe street. This ran for a few more blocks before the car made another right onto MLK Street. MLK was an unpaved road still full of construction gear off to the sides. Giant machines were sanding down the limestone channels on either side.

One final left brought us to Sangita Ave where we beheld: Sangita, a varicolored coral castle of bulbous domes and spires, antennae and balustrades in the Pelutchian style of old Tartaria. And forged of the same indigo stone that matched Mount Typhon, hazily visible through the clouds northwest of Sangita. To the northeast Mount Tiamat's, broken peaks bent overhead like a splayed apart rib cage.

Michael craned his neck peering up at the bending mountains. "How's it doing that?" I gripped his sweating hands and tugged him up the marble steps of Sangita.

"They are not really above us Michael, its just how the land looks to us. From higher up it doesn't look that way," I said. "Look, no shadows, you see?" I tried to show him, but between Mount Typhon, Tiamat and Sangita he seemed unable to factor it all together. Marvelous work by whoever made it.

"Marvelous, indee'dio Madam. Was your travel gentle?" asked a man who stood at the top of the marble steps. He wore a similar armor to Michael's, but his was transparent, glassy, filled with swirls that could not be fire. The colors were various, seguing, seething, as if every color swirled within his body. His face was Hispanic though, a yellow smile, high and tight hair, dark brown eyes, with crows feet and a peppered mustache (that needed a trim). Two silver stripes ran down his shoulders. I say this because I stared him down wondering, *how did he respond to what I just thought?*

Michael put himself between us.

"Would you like a reinstatement *Corporal*? Itching to use those *human* muscles in that government issued armor?"

Michael did not flinch.

"I am Captain Margarito of the Amraken Manticores. My orders are to inform you that only Yuza Moth is welcome in this place. Corporal Lynx and I will have a chat while y'all get reacquainted," he said with a wink.

I glared at this man and said, "You knew my Yalson. He wrote of you. Where is he? I order you to tell me sweeper boy. Yeah, I see you now."

He reached us in three skipping strides from the top to the bottom of the stairs. "Your answers and your son are ahead. Although you will have no peace if you continue."

Michael turned to face him, but the *glamer* of Margarito's armor made him pause.

"Yal is here? *Where?*" I did not wait for a response. I entered Sangita alone.

There are too many details I could try to describe. Sangita had changed much since I birthed Yal somewhere within fifteen years ago.

I was engulfed in an ocean of life. An atrium held all the animals from the murdered land we'd seen. Bison, bobcats, raccoon, horses, pandas and parrots, all the beetles, worms slugs, and eagles; the lizards, manatees, gorillas and elephants, everything, *everything*, but most of all there were hundreds of small cats, frogs and rabbits.

All slumbered in the midst of chatters and snores of Elengen preserved— grasses, shrubs, trees, bamboo, vines and flowers lining trickling streams over mossy stones into ponds teeming with lilies, cattails and varicolored fish. Several moths, awake and moving floated over. I reached out and they landed on me, their colors changing as they sang their ear tickling songs.

"I don't think you would have expected this of me Yuza. Marvelous indeed I would agree." whispered that quicksilver voice I kept hearing.

I turned to look behind me. The moths all fluttered away. A thick pink cloud hung before me, shifting and twisting between warm yellow hues. "It's good you found new love Yuza." whispered the cloud again. "Bastet is among her pride past the pond." The cloud dissipated. When you're ready."

The shifting scents and odors forbade any fear from rising within me. Nothing pulled me, I found my way through the trodden paths of all the sleeping beasts. Along black sand were crocodiles snored with crabs nestled along their bellies. Blips of green flashed from within the pond to reflect an empty, black hole in the center of the ceiling where a ring depicted The Fountainheads in pure color tones. Upon the ring in a clockwise rotation with the roman numerals underneath were:

I, Chrlnimar as a crimson lynx with clocks for eyes. II Posemar as azure serpent. III Skemememar as purple pregnant woman. IV Remar bronze horned person with details stricken away. V Femar as golden man with hammer and t-square in hand. VI Vladomar as bearded face with breasts covered tree for its body. VII Ommamar as silver crest/trough waveform. VIII Temar as orange androgynous youth with two open hands. IX Jehmar as pink animal: hoofed feet, fish tail feathered wings. X Hemar as rough brown sphere with a red grid around it. XI Querinimar as teal rim around an empty mirror. XII Zom as dry gray bones.

My stupor increased a glowing red and blue moths surrounded me. "This way Yuza," whispered Zoe. Silver trails of vapor puffed through the jungle where vines and mushrooms were the carpet of the earth. Across a brook: Bastet, snored with her head against the belly of a white tiger.

I could not hate her. I looked around for my own lion to nap upon. Why wouldn't I?

"Geeze you two," aid Zoe, not whispering this time. Gold light illumined the entire atrium. I turned my eyes away. And a tiny kitten fell into my hands from a small orange cloud before me, "keep hold of her, you need her pheromones to stay safe!" said Zoe.

"Meow!" cried the kitten.

"Bastet!" cried Zoe as the same orange cloud went over and ruffled Bastet's hair wildly.

Several Lions roared.

"Hey!" shouted Bastet.

Several Lions whimpered.

"Zoe!"

"Yuza is here!"

"Huh?" Finally Bastet looked at me.

"Oh…Yuza. How goes?" her dark eyes cracked open, *"Smell the roses yet?"* she crooned. Despite awakening, her hair began to untangle itself and bold, black lines formed underneath her golden eyes.

"Where is Yal?" was all I had to say to her.

My Sister respected me enough to get right to the point. We ended up sitting down in a cat cafe just outside the atrium. Each tile on the floor was a different color with every hue represented. Sunlight streamed in from skylights warming the entire cafe. Wooden walls, chairs, tables and counter tops were all varnished and sparkling. Louis Wain paintings of anthropomorphic cats adorned each pink and blue pastel wall.

The orange kitten in my hands hopped down to greet all the other cats who surrounded Bastet. The small orange cloud followed us and solidified into a humbler, more human appearance of a soft, green cardigan and a long rainbow colored skirt with skin of darkest earth. Zoe hugged me with all the strength and love a sister could. "Don't worry, I'm still me."

I let my older sister cradle me as not even Michael could. She absorbed the tears of my confusion. *What is Zoe? Have I lost myself?*

"We won Yuza and we couldn't have done it without Yal," said Bastet from within her posse of gray Maine-Coons, and calicoes who rubbed their noses along our calves.

"Chai tea?" asked Zoe.

"Yum!" said Bastet.

"Is he safe?" I asked.

"Yes, yes, Yuza you have nothing to worry about. Relax, enjoy your tea," said Bastet.

We three sat and drank our tea as the cats played around us. After awhile, I gathered my will to consider how to approach them. In every way I could not feel the girls I'd grown up with. My eyes could barely reconcile the barrages of sights presented to me. No where could a bare white wall or dormant corner be found. Activity, color, plants, glued in excessive obsession to have no single empty space.

The tea soothed my throat and I found the strength of my own voice.

"Zoe, Bastet, I do not understand what has become of you. I have seen my Son murder another man in front of me. I have seen my Son spared by someone he tried to kill in order to defend me. I have read of his body changing in ways I cannot understand. I have had machines try to collar me for no seeming reason. Life grows from the shedding of our communities first skin. Makeda tells me of victories and losses and yet Yal could not come back home to me with her and the other survivors. I have only these letters. I am pregnant, I cannot carry the weight of three hearts at once. Show me my Son, living or dead."

Bastet scanned me with her golden eyes. Her black hair had straightened, her dress resisted the fluff of the cats at her feet.

"I'll show her, Bastet. That's all she wants."

"Fine, but only remote," Bastet pulled one of the Amraken phones out and tapped on it. The windows shuttered, the lights went out and a beam projected illumined an image of our Earth, but it had these huge lines around it, like a cape of spider legs, instead of only showing the blue marble.

Zoe began, "Every 12,000 years, Sabaoth, the local Sun of our Unkenoma, emits a solar flare that thrashes against the magnetosphere of every planet in our system. That is what all these lines around the Earth mean: magnetosphere.

"Each time this happens Anthropos is all but wiped out, forced to live in caves to survive while the land, sea and air is sundered by the increased surface temperatures and floods from land based ice deposits. We are never able to rebuild ourselves on our own. The fungi had to evolve into our enteric and autonomic nervous system. This symbiosis preserved consciousness alongside our natural instincts to cooperate and ensure survival by any means necessary.

"To observe a person guided by emotion and instinct is to observe, in effect a walking, talking mushroom. *A Slobe.* Life always multiplies again in some form somewhere. This has been happening since Akachi first climbed from Glia's sea-salt slime and divided himself. Whether in our gut, our bread, our wine, in the very fact that forests exist, we are nothing without *Myco's Kingdom.*

"We have no power or recourse. The Sun itself kills all life on the surface and there is nothing anyone can do about it—except Akachi. The oceans boil, but the deep sea actually gets a benefit of increased photons for a time. That stirs up the next batch of archaea and phytoplankton to rise up from the ocean floor. The magnetic poles of our own planet shift. North, south, all of that stops meaning anything. The Sun turns black with massive sunspots and the moon reddens; this is the signal to all that the sun is aiming itself at their world. Sabaoth surges, ejaculates, and smites the magnetosphere of every planet in the solar system with enough force to collapse the atmosphere needed by carbon based life. Only Earth, whose true name is Akamoth, have been able to survive this tyrannical cycle. A direct hit of solar plasma will turn anything it touches into vapor by its flame. All matter that matters, the entire material world is punk for Sabaoth's fire," said Zoe.

"What happened to Yal?" I asked.

Zoe laughed with a polyphony of melodic voices.

"Lets take a closer look then," said Zoe. Still in darkness she led me to the balcony. Above us the fractured moon fragments hovered throughout the local sky. I shrieked at the sight. Abrax...the moon, but I thought it was fine. Why? Wedges, pieces, would they be continent sized if they were closer? They hover in orbit. But that is just me relaying what I saw. I had no words at the time, just groans and moans. Zoe's form still made no sense to me. But this! The moon is broken. *Yal was telling the truth.*

Below us was the North Elengen— where Pelutch had been. From horizon to horizon, extending along newly formed craters, filled with red lakes was a section of a glowing indigo ring jutting out of the broken earth.

Zoe continued, "Akachi survives alone, untouched. And every 12,000 years the Fountainheads give him a list of humans and other species to gather and bring back to Elengen and Pelutch specifically. We are the crop he cuts and threshes and grinds into the meal of his endless feasts. This terrestrial ring, this *Anthrorgan*, built by Akachi for his use alone is what communicates between the Bloodforge of our world's heart, Abrax the moon and Abraxas, the magnetosphere which contains and protects the Earth and Moon from Saboath, the Holy Sun."

Bastet cut in, "Gráinne offered Us, The Moths of Elengen to ensure we would survive without having to be chosen. She lied to us about our progressive opportunities in Elengen. There was never going to be a New Age for us. No reset, awakening or ascension, no rapture, just more sloosh for Akachi's game. Zoe was the first to know and have the means to do something about him. Zoe made the descent through the seven gates to HIM. She was crushed by HIM. He devoured her. She was reborn. And now WE have defeated HIM."

Bastet stepped beside me and grasped my hand with her ice-cold and bejeweled fingers. "Our plan was complicated, but boiled down to convincing the Amraken and Vlaruska warmongers to commit a massive amount of force into one location, destroy each other, and as a side effect, break the seven ancient gates which had been locked up tight for the past 12,000 years.

Once he learned what we were up to Akachi destroyed Pelutch and the Amrakens and the Vlaruskans and every Manticore with his thundering hands. Margarito and I could barely keep pace with him. Yal made all the difference in the end."

"I do not care," was all I could manage to say. The tea had not helped keep me alert. I'se so tired.

"Yuza is the best of us after all," said Zoe.

"Why bring me here? Why show me these horrors? How many lives were lost down there?" I could not hold myself back. "Yal said a million fighters fought here. Pelutch had millions too and dozens arrived with Makeda. You!" I jabbed a finger into the cold, earthen heart of Zoe. "Beyond all reason and comparison you call yourself life itself while you alone are beyond death. Is this the cost that you two alone decided to pay? Cui bono? Millions of souls lost—show me my boy—please." I finally collapsed and Zoe swerved to catch me. I had nothing left to hold onto, Zoe was thin as air. I wept like a terrified girl. I am sure Bastet enjoyed that since she stepped back from me, her perfect pedicured purple toes immune to the dust of the dead in the air.

Zoe remained with me. "Yuza, I am no longer human. I can only feign what the old Zoe might've done. Without my flesh I have no emotions. I can see how you hurt. The same way I listened to all the cries of the dying millions of this valley. I sat with each one as much as I could. They pleaded with me, called me Akamoth herself in the name by which they knew her. They prayed to her, to me, to the Fountainheads and at the end to Akachi for salvation or at least silent damnation. Neither he nor I could offer that. Humanity is a hyper-organism called Anthropos, a fusion of fungus and mammalian D.N.A. that functions like a sort of mobile fruiting bodysuit for mycelial networks. I am made of spores and radio waves, a Vapor-Fractal, a Post-Human. That which has been sought by every generation of man. True immortality, not a deity reliant on faith and prayer. I am that which was dreamed of in all those spindly stone carvings and statues and cave paintings mistaken as electricity, serpents or worms."

We are mycelium.
MYCO
We taught trees how to have roots.
Without them, Akachi would still be slime in the
ocean.
It's always been fungi,
our kingdom is
rhizomes,
all the way down.

"And I, Zoe, am the first to fuse Akamoth and the best technology of Amraken, Vlaruska and Pelutch into one new form. The twelve colored mushroom spores and blocks you have seen— is and was me Yuza. I have have been with you all this time. Yal, the best of Akachi's Amraken–Elengen brood, was the key. For all the terrors around us. Yal was the spitting image of Akachi. And—"

"You sacrificed him!" I clawed at the moist air of her vapor body in futility.

"He made a choice that no other Man could. Not even Margarito managed what Yal has. Look, I will guide your eyes." The moist air coalesced into a teal tunnel filled with mirrors right in front of my eyes.

I finally saw my one time lover and my son. Akachi was mounted atop my Yal—same as he had mounted all of the Moths. Both with golden manes. Both with bared fangs. Yal had no lines between flesh, steel, plant, glass or stone. Akachi, his eagle wings broken, while otherwise pure stone indigo. His black bloodied hands held my boy's throat. Spittle

117

had frozen between Akachi's blue tongue and Yal's exposed chrome shoulder bones. Both their eyes were glassy and filled with an everycolored fire. Yal's single human hand bypassed a barrier of lavender glass. In that hand was a humble chalice, filled with the same everycolored glow as Yal and Akachi's eyes.

My Yal became manticore; he finally met *his idol, his god, his father, the Man Eternal: Akachi, Tyrant of Elengen.*

The cloud of this vision dispersed. The entire sky began to swirl. The mountains rumbled. A thin pink fog flowed over the dead and broken land. The sky opened up a bit and violet rays broke through all of the gray. These colors, this vapor, coalesced into a larger and larger varicolored cloud.

"This is not magic Yuza. I speak and the atoms and elements listen. I am that I am."

The clouds thickened into four indigo wings. A bloody orb drips from the center. This heart cracks and rainbow veins surged through its wings. On each wing four golden orbs opened.

"You are the mother of a hero Yuza. Your son accomplished what no Man ever has. Accept your honor and raise your Daughter in peace. I am here and everywhere that life is. The island is under our wings now." said Zoe: The Great Moth of Elengen.

Part 5: Aktaly, the Little Moth

02/14/1992

It's Aktaly's Birthday!

All of our mothers live on through you
Kingdoms of the small world: dirt, spores and seeds
Tell all who meet you, the Vaporflame is felt, not seen
All of our fathers live on through you
Life itself has evolved beyond anyone's ken
You have a chance to be self-defined in this new world

You were the seed of my field
All of my life was transformed for you
Loss of your smile will never be forgot

My
Ignorant
Cute
Husband
And
Everlasting
Lifeboat

May we find
Ontology
Through
Hell

I see you.
You are real.
I have made you.
In the light your eyes are teal like your Amraken
Father
In the dark your eyes are pink like your Elengen
Mother
Your lush hair denies one colored label
I see every path you will take.
You will be tall and clever
You will write your own life song.
I will fight for every path you step upon.
So you may find your heart's true desire.
You have been the pause between my heartbeats for
these nine months.
I hear you still, with only a single breaths delay.
Through the Vaporflame we will always be connected
we are both its fuel, its humble punk.
All the generations, some four thousand pairs have all
led to YOU;
same as any human life, no matter how mighty or
meager.
Your Father and I are the only ones who celebrate you.
Felicia is asleep in the next bed over. She's expecting
her own daughter any day now. Gráinne barely moves
anymore, Makeda has too many people who need her.
Bastet did not bother. Amraken life keeps them busy,
but we, your parents are together for you, my Aktaly.
We'll be together everyday now.
Your teal myco-fiber clothes will never wear out,
they will clean themselves and grow with you.
You will never have to fear heat or cold.
Zoe Moth, Goddess of this new world visits
I tell her my human daughter rises to meet her.
You are more than your namesake.
You are more than our daughter
You are Aktaly Moth
And you can be whoever you want to be.

4/13/1992

Dear Aktaly, the Pelutch Quarter fence is no more, replaced by the fence around the ziggurat construction site. Which is being quarried out from Tia-Tara and the hills surround to make room for The Zarden: a fancy new fifteen minute super building. *How many hills have been hollowed in pursuit of something believed to exist deep within the dirt, while feigned identical to the glamer of the projection in the architects mind?*

I tell no one of what I know. If I had not written I would have forgotten already myself. Bastet programs our culture through Sangita, which she calls a school. Zoe is unknown to all while active everywhere. I see her wispy form gliding, connecting, observing and whispering. No one goes hungry, no one will die of thirst, no one will ever be alone on Elengen ever again.

Not even Yal.

Yet I sit around friends, my new family, in our widening circles on our 3D printed to look like hand woven mats, and I can no longer feel the presence of other bodies warmth. Michael stays with me as much as he can, but its mostly you and me now. I feel every beating of your heart. I live for you.

I must tell you to not be like me Aktaly. Humans have little time left to live, once you can, if you ever read this, just live your fucking life. Don't listen to any boys, any men, any influencers, or pop idols or gurus on the web and don't listen to any bitches or hoes either. Listen to me, this one time. Even if we fight, I die, or if Sabaoth burns us all beyond infinity.

Never stop loving yourself because no one is able to love you more than you can love yourself. Only your own heart will never leave you.

I was a person before I was a mother. I had my own starry dreams of designing a stage play rendition of Orpheus and Eurydice. I wanted to see her and Persephone both escape Hades on their own with Hecate's help. I wanted girls to write their own lines for their own roles and not be supplanted by squeaky choir boys. Gráinne didn't know what to do with me, other than try to make me into a copy of her. I won't get in your way, but I also will not be there often in the way you will need me either. You will grow up without knowing there is a difference between Amraken and Elengen peoples since that is what everyone who remains is now.

I wonder though, what if we can't do it? No Human would truly desire to be a god or goddess. Zoe is no longer Human though, how will she shape this new world? Will she rename us to an artifice of her choosing? Will she re-compose all that has been decomposed?

Slow and steady, steady and slow we shall persevere through this Vaporspore Aeon. Like picking tomatoes, cotton, keeping families together, bands in tune, or writing cursive. I know we'll figure things out. Our gardens grow. Michael's back with a resonator guitar and a chapbook on yodeling. He's been practicing with the Pelutchians to learn Melodica dub. Bastet asked me to have him look out for Spryaig. She wanted her boy to have at least one decent man to look up to. We'll see...

[Later, around midnight]

I had a dream, rare for me, but I think having you with me all the time has done more good for me than I'll ever know. At first you were a belief to hold my soul together. Now you are a living person and I must hold your soul together, until you can do it for yourself.

I dreamed of you as an adult standing against Akachi who's presence will never leave Elengen. Spryaig, Dio and Zani are all his final children. Bastet and Makeda have carried their honor and our shame intertwined with the sweat of their brows and the blood shed for no one. I see you all, healthy, alongside a new generation of Elengen. I suspect Felicia's newborn Maria is Yal's child and Bastet has her own second son Remus with Margarito.

Imagine yourself as I dreamed you, unless you can come up with something better. This may be me projecting, but I see no harm innit. Some role model is better than none for most of us anyway. The colors of my dream were teal and indigo, with barely any crimson between the two of you. The Girl and the God, Aktaly and Akachi, however unlikely as this may be. You are separate from him, you do not carry his blood. Amraken, through your Father and I, is born anew, rather than reproduced in you.

You said, "Damned lies have been carved into stone and the stones themselves shall revolt against this. Without compassion all debts and taxes will amount to biomass for our own funeral pyres with vapor replacing our souls. Ignorance has been preferred to awareness, outrage has been preferred to empathy and comfort has tried to replace beauty."

And Akachi, whispering through thunder and sleeping breaths said, ***"You will chill. You will desire. You will fade. You will sleep. You will not dream. You will beg for the mystery of my absence Moths. Yes, I see you, flying amok and in your cocoons. We will decompose and re-compose you. There will be a long, cold, whisper of murmuring cells, waiting for conditions to align and begin a biological race all over again— the primal war of attrition and nutrition— entropy, WAR by any other name.***

"I will outlast you as I have done to countless brats like you before. Such is the Unkenoma, awe-striking rot of nature; wrought by the eternal will of the Vaporflame which I nearly snuffed out."

And then you said, *"No, Akachi. You did not compose this world which has no beginning; it is repeating tones and selecting octaves beyond your taxonomy. Vibrate, resonate, punk, before entropy, pulls even you into a vaporous spiraling embrace."*

And *I* said:
Seek the Vaporflame in all that you do
Evolve like an Elengen Moth
Do not fragment like Abrax
or Sabaoth will burn you
and Akachi will devour you
while Abraxas observes you
Die and be reborn like Akamoth;
and you will become such dung that Old Beetle will be pushing
into yet *another* Neo-Babylon.

05/09/2001

Dear Aktaly, you and your mother are sound asleep. There ain't much noise beyond the drone of the window A/C and the murmuring reruns of *The Prisoner* on TV. This peace, this quiet is its own reward Aktaly. Never reward yourself for anything before you've done the thing you're rewarding yourself for. Too many fools, fellas, all kinds of people who get stressed or excited and drop their given pleasures in lots of little doses, sips, drags, pops, patches and sniffs. Treating themselves like dogs, rewarding themselves between every panting breath. I hope you'll understand what I mean when.

I figured I could give you a glimpse of my day, today would do plenty fine. Let you see a slice of your Father's life. Won't be the same kinda lesson as your Mom was trying to show you about how she handled those early, transitional years.

At first these journals were handed out to gauge the populations sentiments and compose social action profiles. I'se part of the Amraken invasion force in 1991. When my platoon landed we had a whole dossier of targets but most of the profiles were empty. The Amraken–Elengen people like Gráinne, Felicia, and your Mother, and the Native Elengen, the Pelutchians like Makeda and all her people weren't turning the journals in to their liaisons. Zoe was the change agent for Yuza's area, Tara, think it was— that hill the Zarden was built out of anyway.

And thank goodness for *you*! And for *me* since my squad was sent to clear the homesteads that had profiles labeled something no human being should ever be labeled. That already had my bullshit detector blaring that something was off about our orders. I didn't know what was going on at the time.

Tekbros loosed the truth easy while drinking up at the *Scaly Pear* often enough. Place was a mock dive bar trying to copy a Texas Bar by someone who never been by the looks of the complimentary cowboy hats they'd hand out at the front door. Reckon I'm getting distracted telling you things that won't mean anything to ya until your older. The point was your Mother kept her journal, wrote it all addressed to you, I found it in the trunk of my car and I'm not going to read another word that wasn't meant for me.

I will add my own little letter to your Mother's though. I don't write much other than for work invoices or somesuch, but let's see what we get.

My daily routine ended when I found this notebook in the back of my Pontiac. I think I've scrambled time a bit much already. Here, I'll set you straight by going right from the top.

I always wake at 5:42am, right before a silent *Reverie.* I knew in my sleep something was about to happen and I'd wake up ahead of it so it wouldn't surprise me and such. Hope that makes sense. I go and check on the both of yous. Then, I chugged a quart of water and went for a jog around the Quarter. I made mental notes of any stray dogs, wandering drunks, varicolored moths, and growing cracks in the streets, sidewalks and asphalt lots. I think it's good mental practice to note changes around our Home. It's automatic for me.

I didn't realize I'se doing it until Yuza called me out one morning when she joined me. Your Mother is an incredible woman Aktaly. Smartest person I ever met and only you will surpass her Beauty.

I never know when another Amraken surprise will be popping up among the winos and lot lizards. Those poor fellas though, doped up, sweating out the spirits while showering in fiery gold. Let them be a lesson that that could be any one of us after a few too many bad days when safety nets become too safe.

The Guards at the PX would leave the broom out for me at one end of the strip mall. I'd leave it at the other end by Tyger's. I'd sweep the sidewalk in front of each store except the PX and Tyger's place. The PX is a sorta generic looking concrete Amraken hub for the remains of the Army and the Pelutchians once they made peace with each other. Only place to get and send airmail out by VTOL or drone.

Only a few hundred Amrakens are left. Mostly civilians, engineers, service workers, all without supply lines from the mainland. Pelutchians know the Island through and through. They took the lead in every area. Neo-Babylon might as well be Pelutch 2.0. I'm lucky I married your Ma when we did. All the Amrakens now are the minority demographic and the origin of this whole city is tied up to what my kind did to theirs. I still try to wrap my head around that one. Even a decade later some people on both sides just don't wanna settle for better and get good and right along. Folks like your Ma and I ended up being the real liaisons between cultures. How much of the worst coulda been avoided if leadership had just been up front about what the war was even for?

Tyger though, already'd be up, blanching bacon, getting his fryers and grills all set. His family grown out to have three boys and five daughters and they'd all already started on families of their own. We'd nod, speak somedays or not at all. Today Tyger called me over to ask me how the families doing and if I'd seen Kurshanabi yet. Tyger's been houndin' for some debts the Old Ferryman owed him for food and tack from right before the invasion!

I tell him that y'all doing fine, that you'll be starting school soon, that Yuza's still holding herself together about Gráinne's—*she'll get better*—is what I told him. He nodded, scratching silver hairs around his cauliflower ears, "Shame that. Damn shame. You tell the Kursh when you silo him. Now git."

I laid the broom by the dumpsters alongside Tyger's and headed out, through the morning fog mixed with wood smoke. For all the effing solar panels riddlin' the Quarter and Neo-Babylon beyond, none of it did a lick of squick under consistent cloud cover— *or at night.* The cold, dewy air stuck to me but that didn't bother me as much as other Amraken green boys. They're still coping with their skin suits and central air. Come night they burn wood like anyone else when that's all we have.

From about 6am to 9am I work in a garage along with whoevers in there needin' work done. Cars, trucks, scooters, bicycles, rollie-shoes, carts, hand wagons, electric loaders, small diesel tractors, leaf blowers—anything with wheels or motors whether gas, lithium-ion, hydrogen or pneumatic. The garage was built out of the bottom floor of another of them concrete block towers the Amrakens loves to *squeeze* out. Look at me, referring to my own people as 'Amrakens' **No,** I've chosen my side— **_I'm a Moth_** now. A father. A husband. A soldier <u>no longer.</u>

Your Mom gets you ready in the morning and I'd drop you off at Sangita for School. They're easy going about tardiness so it ain't much of a thing, but back in my day being on time meant something important so I always get you to school right at 10am sharp.

Next I'd get stuck in Neo-Babylon's midday rush hour as all the Amraken office workers rocket around the roads to get to work by 11am and lunch at noon. My 1969 GTO Judge Pontiac has a steel chassis. I wasn't worried about any of these *Tekbros* on their scooters and e-bikes running into *me* or smearing the car's teal and white trim. I did have concern about running into *them* and getting sued though. I only dealt with it all because I had to pick up Spryaig. He's a young man now and he's earned a chip on his shoulder. Unlike most young guns firing blind, the things Spryaig engineers actually work.

Yuza and Bastet made a deal way back about making sure Spryaig had at least one decent male role model in his life. I understand that well enough to not ask why *I* had to be the one to do it. Saddlin' a handyman with chauffeur duty doesn't make much sense to me, but its a job. I guess I am his uncle.

Maybe its about Yal, *poor kid*. Although I do wonder sometimes about Maria, Felicia's daughter, since she doesn't look like Floyd. What're the odds Maria is actually Yal's daughter like Yuza says?

Today Spryaig and I loaded some petrified bones and sacks of roots, tendrils, and crimson *chrln* tines into pelican cases. I tried to ask whats what, but he'd be wrapped up in his headset. I followed his itinerary from Sangita for the day.

Our first stop was a construction crew out east. The desalination ponds were built where the Elengen use to grow blue corn, red beans, and watermelons.

All made of this new graphcrete stuff that could be grown and shaped. Same as the Moths old Taradome. The salty, acrid air fogged my car windows. Fellas in bio-chem suits patrol the ponds to vacuum up anything that leaks over the edges. Your Ma had a role in that'n. I think about the time she was pregnant with ya. when was that? Sure she wrote about that but I won't rifle through these pages anymore than I already have. Yuza she had a bad infection for awhile after the hyper-saline landed on her. They gave her anti-parasitics and anti-fungals for that though. I'm no doctor, I can't speculate. Spryaig mighta' known if I'd asked him.

We pulled up to a bare upturned rib cage flexing in the wind like a broken, heaving chest. Think it used to be called Mount Tiamat. While Mount Typhon, opposite us, pierced the sky with its steep indigo faces. A crew of Pelutchians and Amrakens were aiming large building machines with computers and joysticks to place the lattice work for an above ground rail line over the entire eastern industrial zone. Both 'races' of men were multi-colored. Maybe iron blueberry as Yuza'd say, maybe lavender, maybe every type of soil from gray through brown and obsidian. Maybe periwinkle pink, saturnine green, blue sometimes, yellow lots, red, reddish orange. Neither type of man was ever white or black.

Spryaig and I waited as workmen pulled the packages from the trunk. *(Forgive me Judge, I'll get it buffed out. I promise Judge.)* Speakin' of someone who likes to dictate. Spryaig gives the worst a run to the stars to escape his whinging lectures. I've told him I don't understand most of what he says. I think he thinks out loud or something. He does not repeat himself. He does not ask if I understand. This was one bit I pulled from my car's audio recorder ***(for his own insurance purposes of recordings of his musings as a commodity.)***

"The rails are built with 'reinforced bamboo combined with myco-electronic inoculated graphcrete. The buildings will live. The city will live. Live, live, eyes in every wall. Where do the vending machines, compilers compactors, where? Are they essential? Footsteps measured between purchase in-home vs communal—do calorie exchanges levy out? Within the rail-cars! Yes, yes, YES. Fuel? Biomass? Decomposer to velocity? Hmm Hmm Hmm. Yes!"

He kept on like that talking through his helmet as I drove to our next stop. We passed through the eastern industrial zone full of septic facilities, solar fields, power substations for the geothermal + hydro-electric interconnect. Wind turbines were silent and under maintenance further north of the desalination fields. All under a maroon overcast that would not break.

At the next sight we could get out and breathe clear around Zofya's Lake, northwest of Sangita.

Where the same Amraken and Elengen crews were manning machines to build a new dam and canal.

The air reminded me of the Rockies back in Amraken—a sip of crisp ice cold water while sweating, while wearing five layers against 10 degree temperatures on hikes with my aunts and cousins, or later with my squad training in the mountains. Elengen's hills were not so high as the Rockies, but there wasn't much difference in perspective. Legions of pipes and frames and tanks cover most of what I could see. Sangita, like a mutant cauliflower stands out of course. Neo-Babylon's bending towers emerge from the industrial hearth. The Zarden's lights don't work half the time.

The Pelutch Quarter and the annex quarters south of the river still look like places people might be. Squeezed between all that is forest south of the city. The maroon overcast would not break as airships misted lime green coolant onto the vertical frankencorn farms everywhere else.

I wouldn't believe that progress could be so nightmarish if I hadn't seen similar such before. I enlisted after my hometown became a company town for a frankencorn corporation. It's rare to step on soil anymore in the city limits. Asphalt, concrete, kaliche, glassed desert and deforested miles of ash— which my old Army boots were all rated for.

We trekked up some dusty stairs to an observation room built on stilts. More Tekbros inside. Here they would remove their headsets. Spryaig was pale with a fuzzy mustache and uneven sideburns. His eyes were pure gold though. Once I got him there my part was done. Told you it was senseless, unless there was something else going on I didn't understand.

3–4pm I'd meet Yuza in the food court at the Zarden. She worked in the Superstore at a library co-working place. We'd both get some rabbit food from the cafeteria. I'd chew and listen to her tell me about her day. The familiarity of this was good for us both I think. '91 was a hard year for everyone. We found some decent routines after you were born. Good for all of us I'm hoping. She has her own car, a 2000 red Geo Metro hatchback. After work she checks in with Gráinne over at the hospital. I'd pickup you up from school about 5pm.

Salads were good yea, but I'm an Amraken and I love my fried food. After chatting with Yuza I'd leave the Zarden and stroll down to the *Scaly Pear* for a some greasy, fried chicken wings and lemonade. And I'd got down to licking the last of the chili garlic sauce from my fingers when Sgt. Floyd done sat next to me at the bar.

"Caught your bird eh Lynx?"

"This time," I said.

"Yous guys d'n wawkin' on mah cah?"

"Slippin' Floyd. Slippin'"

He shakes his bald red head while rubbing his brown curly beard then orders two pints of imported Bavarian beer. Bartender poured them out with lots of just the right amount of foam.

Floyd held his up waiting for me to clang glasses. I just stared at the air bubbles floating in that foamy yellow, carbonated poison.

"What the f**k is wrong with you?" Floyd asked.

I looked him straight in the eyes and said, "I have to pick up our Daughters from school."

His brow furrowed, his eyes twitched. He chugged his whole pint in a few gulps, then chucked it right past my ears into a corner bin. The glass did not break. Some droplets, spittle, did land on my cheeks and neck though.

"You think you're smart do ya?"

I checked the time on a TV above the bar showing football game replays. I had to get going and I'se sure arguing with Floyd about the merits of not drinking alcohol would not help either of us much. We use to drink a lot back in the day, before and during my stint in the Army. I had an Elengen wife and daughter; Floyd had an Elengen wife and daughter.

I got up and left, without another word, only an offered handshake. Floyd chugged the second pint and threw it at me after I opened the door to leave. That glass did break right out on the sidewalk. A sign of Pelutchian ingenuity, a roaming trash collect'n robot swept up the shards before anyone could step on them.

I was there for you and Maria right on time— I like to be early, but on time is better than late. The school was mixed, weren't many young folk or adults still bothering to learn, lotta them just worked there doing who knows what. Most people were not parents. Most Amrakens were silos, without families.

The older Pelutchian kids like Makeda's son Dio and others too, all kept near the few real youngins' like you, Maria, Zani and Remus. The only four faces on the in South Elengen with their own unique colors. You four carry the potential of this whole island's future in your little hands and backpacks. Remus might be an ethical Spryaig or an even worse one. Maria might become a bigot or a role model. Zani, is already taller than her older brother Dio and she's learned the names of all the flowers left on Elengen. And you, *Aktaly*, you have both of your parents. Hopefully our Love will not confuse you while you tread your own path in YOUR homeland.

I watched the road, stayed silent and listened as you, Zani and Maria talked. I took the scenic southwest route through the Forest of Cats en route back to Floyd and Felicia's place off Pump Street. Y'all love spotting all the cats and tryna name 'em. Big cats, small cats, tiny cats and a few inland sea-lions. All chilling around a watering hole. Birds were the same such by size, swaying around and chirping.

Downstream slept crocodiles while crabs and tortoises made their given ways across the black, sandy stream banks. Zani points out the flowers when y'all ask her to name one or dozens. Sharpest six year old I ever seen. I'm really glad? I don't know the right word for this feeling Aktaly. Having good, smart friends is almost as important for a kid as having a safe and loving home.

Kids gotta live in four worlds at once. **The world of being a child to parents.** Whether they are there or not its a biological world we get born into right? ***The world of being a young person in the spheres of other young people…or not. What're words if you got no one to speak or listen to? The world of being a human being in a world, increasingly bereft of humanity.*** Literally and uh…figure uh—what's the word? *I don't know, and that's okay. And this is part of the problem—*not enough folks willing to simply say 'I don't know' and own it without shame. ***Most of all though, we all live in our own world.*** Like ere'body does, seeing ourselves half reflected by others back to us and half, all in our own little heads. All your feelings, tastes, memories, and *wounds* will always be yours and everyone you shared them with. You will always be the one who awakens to and survives each day.

When we dropped Maria off at home, Felicia waved from the front door as Maria climbed the stairs to their smart home condo. Floyd's motorcycle was absent from his private parking spot at the base of the stairs. The spot was tripled, three spots combined. Little, red haired Maria passed through the dark yard. I put the car into park and looked around. I started to reach for my...then I seen Maria reach Felicia at the top of the stairs and all my storming blood slowed to a cool, calm trickle.

We were driving home with Zani when the Judge overheated and I had to pull over—no oil. I gathered Aktaly with her backpack. She had her little toy keyboard in her bag, but the batteries were out. Figured as much. Zani didn't mind the sun. She helped me make a little hoodie for Aktaly from two teal work shirts.

We trekked down the highway about three quarters of a mile until we came to a SlickTaco. A new place, looked liked a merger of a SlickQuick and a taco place. Some stupid orange cricket with a seaweed cape was their logo. Probably some Pacifican start up. Zani seemed like a teen already as she went and got her own stuff. I just took it as it was and didn't think any more of it. Anyways, I had enough cash to buy some liter water bottles, for us and my car. And batteries for your little keyboard.

As for the oil— an Amraken fella with a Dallas Cowboys ball cap behind the counter tellin' me "Creep!" when I asked for some Castro-STP 5W–30. I gave 'em the crazy eye until he pointed at the TV hanging from the wall behind me. Stone Temple Pilots playing 'Creep' unplugged at the Black Cube Garden in Old Babylon, Amraken; a replay of the Nov 7 World Bloodbowl halftime show of 1994. The Giants had eaten half the Cowboys that game, if I recall, the Cowboys still won though with their stars crimson forever after. Or was that from the cartoon *Manticore Joe?*

One woman stepped up to me when she saw me lead Aktaly to the bathroom. Asking me what I thought I was doing with her. I'd never considered somebody ever ask a Father some shit like that. I didn't go in with her, just showed her where the bathroom was. While I'm standing there I told her, "She's my Daughter." Then I realized I didn't need to explain myself to the woman. I shut my mouth and waited, ignoring the woman's banter.

Funny thing though, after we got back to the car and got it running again we came back to the gas station for gas. Some cops had showed up and the ole' bitty had curdling blood in her eyes. After an hour and some phone calls the cops left. The woman did not apologize. Instead, with the police driving into the sunset, she spat at me, and called me things I will not repeat. *Some people man.* That was nothing new to me, but Aktaly had never heard those words around her before. She didn't like how the woman yelled, with her razor scrawl of a voice and her wiggling, red tipped fingers. All so unnecessary.

142

We ended up back at Tyger's for dinner. His burger joint was situated such that, as one'd come up the hill from the west, Tyger's original food truck turned billboard blocked the view of the brick and mortar, *Green Castle* slider place over in Glass Town. Ever the clever Tyger and still making burgers like they's back in 1985. I had a double burger with onions rings and hot mustard with pickles. Zani had grilled fish fillets, cabbage and fry bread. Aktaly wanted chicken nuggets, but they didn't have none of those. That Tyger though, he went and cut up a quarter chicken, removed the bones and fried them up, just for you. He even let ya try all of the sauces, to see which one you'd like. You chose honey mustard, made with local honey. How about that? *Local.* I didn't know things were moving in more than one direction. Guess I don't know everything. A good man that Tyger though, a real, good man. Makeda showed up with Dio while we were eating. They'd been at a parent teacher meeting or something. Zani went home with her family.

We got home and watched some bootleg VHS tapes about flying cats and fell asleep. Well, I did for about two hours. I woke up after your Mom had come home and tucked you in. You are sweeter than any cherubic angel. You took a liking to your teal hoodie. I'll make sure to get it upgraded so it grows with you like the rest of your stuff.

I spoke of the worlds that you live in Aktaly. Of this Elengen, for all the different things it is to ere'body here. As your Father my utmost concern is how ***I live in your world.*** I share in the responsibility that is your life. What I do or don't is yours forever. I know—I feel, have felt, continue to feel what its like to wait for someone to help who never shows and who yells at you for your own pain along with whatever else is on their mind. I know what it means to have no one to ask for help when you need it. I almost forgot how to ask for help, even once I'd learned how.

People are people anywhere though. The bullies are the scared, depressed, angry kids who got someone at home breathing down their own neck or worse. The attention seekers are the neglected, they just want friends, but they might get jealous easy. The quiet ones have the most to say, but are used to not having anyone to talk to, listen to them and they'll show you ***hidden worlds of their own.*** I tell you 'bout those, because our instincts tell us those types are 'different' which to our monkey brains anything different is *'food'* or *'bad'* and it makes life harder for everybody. Floyd was a bully, look where that got him. This might not make much sense to you until your older. Everything changes.

I also live in the world of Akachi. On the TV I see all his terrible weapons in countless hands that no army can stand against. Rumors of a

144

whispering wind, guiding storms is a story passing through the WLAN scatterweb socials. Islands vanish, new islands form, thousands day by day. Where does the land go? All that remains is mere vapor. Yuza says its something called *Zoe*, but isn't that just the Greek word for life? Aktaly, **what is this world** I've helped bring you into? It wasn't just me who did this though. Because **there is only one world**, where everyone has a mother. Even if she hurts more than she heals.

You are a Human Being. Yuza wrote this notebook for you. Even before you were born you were guiding her and holding her hands and shoulders as the struggled through those early years while carrying you within her. She wrote this to you, for you, it is yours to have, to read, to destroy, to continue if you choose to.

I'm going to put my pen down now and be glad I was there for my Aktaly. You are safe in your warm bed. Cocooned in your teal hoodie and blankets. Today was a good day. Goodnight. Sweet dreams.

The Moths of Elengen will always be here in these pages for you.

Thank you for reading The Moths of Elengen. Follow me at **akamoth.com.**

The whole story line is planned out and mostly written. I decided to release the first few parts as novellas until I can get enough money for an editor to help me make them all into full novels. I'd like to get into fully produced audiobooks, like radio dramas, but I'd need some help for all that.

I had to write, edit, revise, design, format, publish, archive, and market this whole book by myself. Books are awesome! And this is also one of the most difficult things I've ever done.

I've been working on the story world of the characters introduced in "The Moths of Elengen" since 2010. I produced one short film called "Spryaig" over 2017-2020, which featured some of the elements of this story world for the first time. "The Moths of Elengen" is the proper introduction to the world of *Akamoth*.

Check out the sequels and the film on my website at

akamoth.com

16 years after Zoe Moth's ascension over the patriarchal Akachi in the novella, ***The Moths of Elengen***, a generation of daughters: Aktaly, Zani, Maria, struggle to come of age and keep Elengen folk music alive in Neo-Babylon.

Bastet Moth, Director of the Sangita Institute, maintains a strict regimen for Spryaig, a radical bio-hacker to unlock the secrets of Zoe's immortality. Despite his experiments threatening to accelerate a biological singularity.

As the limits of D.N.A. become fully unlocked, humans, Post-Humans, artificial intelligence, plants, animals and bacteria alike
all evolve
during
Zoe Moth's
VaporSpore Aeon.